SIX FEET UNDER^{SM}

BETTER LIVING THROUGH DEATH

SIX FEET UNDER^{SM}

BETTER LIVING THROUGH DEATH

Edited by Alan Ball and Alan Poul

With contributions by

ALAN BALL · SCOTT BUCK · CARA DIPAOLO · GABE HUDSON · JOANNA LOVINGER
NANCY OLIVER · JILL SOLOWAY · CRAIG WRIGHT

ALAN BALL INTRODUCTION

The first encounter with death that I remember is when our family dog, a nervous brown dachshund named Fritzi, was run over by our next-door neighbor. She was sleeping underneath his car and was crushed when he pulled out of his driveway. I didn't see it happen. I didn't know who disposed of her body or how it was done, but instinctively I understood I shouldn't ask about it. Death was something secretive, mysterious, frightening, better left alone and not observed too closely. Fritzi was just *gone*, soon to be replaced by a new dog, Butch, whom my father said was half chow, which explained his partially black tongue.

I had always said my prayers at bedtime, mechanically droning "If I should die before I wake" like the good little boy I was, without ever really considering what those words meant. They were just singsong phrases that seemed to please the adults, easily memorized, oddly comforting in their ritual repetition. But after Fritzi's mysterious demise, "die" began its gradual evolution from vague concept to something real, something that would one day happen to me and those I loved. We would all just *disappear*. I remember crying fiercely, not so much for Fritzi—we never really cry *for* the dead—but for myself, for my suddenly lost sense of permanency. I asked my mother what was going to happen to me when she and my father died. She smiled and hugged me, and assured me nothing like that would happen for a very long time.

When I was thirteen years old, my sister Mary Ann was driving me to my piano lesson when she pulled out from a blind intersection into the path of an oncoming car. It slammed into her side of our 1973 Ford Pinto, breaking her neck and killing her instantly and cleanly slicing my life in two: everything before the accident, and everything after. And the brief, eternal instant between those two lives where old, familiar possibilities end forever, and new, unimagined possibilities are painfully born.

Death *is* life: an epic, primal force that terrifies and fascinates us, gives our experiences meaning, and ultimately consumes us. As Thomas Lynch puts it: Life goes on, but we don't.

About a year ago I found some old home movies from the early 1960s. I knew they were of family vacations in Indian Rocks Beach, Florida, and I knew my sister would be in them, along with my chain-smoking father, who died of lung cancer six years after she did. I was terrified to watch these faded memories, convinced it would be too painful and send me spiraling into despair (hey, nothing like an early encounter with death to heighten one's sense of drama). But when I finally did watch, I was surprised by how little it affected me. There was my sister, looking chubbier and less graceful than I remembered, irritated at being filmed as she lay on the sand, slick with baby oil and iodine, frying in the sun. And my father, smiling and waving his ever-present cigarette; the really weird part was realizing his middle-aged body looked exactly like the body I see reflected in the mirror every morning as I get out of the shower. There was my mother, younger, happier. And there was me, cheerfully oblivious to everything. It all felt weirdly familiar, but more like a déjà vu than an actual memory of an actual experience.

I have my sister's high school ring, and my father's pocketknife. I have letters she wrote me after she went away to college. I have a wallet, hand-stitched by him out of imitation alligator hide and lined with our kitchen wallpaper from the early 1960s. I have cards and letters and photographs and videotapes of my friends Greg and Janet and Michael. As Ruth Fisher says, "I'm surrounded by relics of a life that no longer exists." But relics are essential. What else do we have to remember someone by? What else can we do but touch something they once wore, made, wrote? How else do we reach our loved ones who are gone but whom we still love, and will never stop loving, even though they stopped loving us?

This book is a collection of just such relics—albeit fictional ones left behind by fictional characters, but to me, these characters are very real. I realize some might view this as a form of madness, and they'd be right. I've been lucky enough to work with some equally mad people on this book—people whose madness I greatly respect—and in the process they have given me a deeper understanding of the Fishers and those with whom their lives are and will always be inextricably bound.

CARLOS CASTANEDA   TALES OF POWER

Without the awareness of

ordinary, trivial. It is only

us that the world is an un

death, everything is
because death is stalking
fathomable mystery.

related to _____
relationship with _ _ _ _
work relationship _ _ _ _ _ _ _ _

1995

VANESSA SUAREZ ——————— + ——————— FEDERICO DIAZ -
1974–   1974–

JULIO DIAZ   AUGUSTO DIAZ
1996–   2001–

2002

LISA (KIMMEL) FISHER ——————— + ——————— NATHANIEL (NATE) FISHER JR.
1967–2003   1965–

MAYA FISHER
2002–

1967

BERNARD CHENOWITH ——————— + ——————— MARGARET CHENOWITH
1943–2003   1945–

WILLIAM (BILLY) CHENOWITH   BRENDA CHENOWITH
1971–   1969–

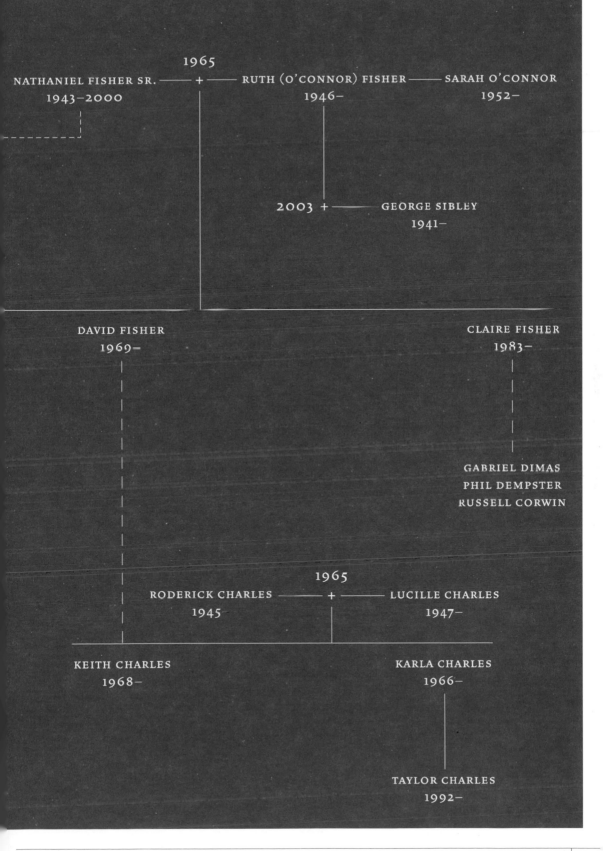

1965

NATHANIEL FISHER SR. ———— + ———— RUTH (O'CONNOR) FISHER ———— SARAH O'CONNOR
1943–2000   1946–   1952–

2003 + ———— GEORGE SIBLEY
1941–

DAVID FISHER   CLAIRE FISHER
1969–   1983–

GABRIEL DIMAS
PHIL DEMPSTER
RUSSELL CORWIN

1965

RODERICK CHARLES ———— + ———— LUCILLE CHARLES
1945–   1947–

KEITH CHARLES   KARLA CHARLES
1968–   1966–

TAYLOR CHARLES
1992–

1941 | THE FISHER & SONS FUNERAL HOME IN LOS ANGELES IS ESTABLISHED BY NATHANIEL'S FATHER.

Fisher & Sons

FUNERAL HOME

2302 West Twenty-fifth Street, Los Angeles, Calif. 90018

1965 | NATHANIEL FISHER, AGE 22, MEETS RUTH O'CONNOR AND MARRIES HER SHORTLY THEREAFTER.

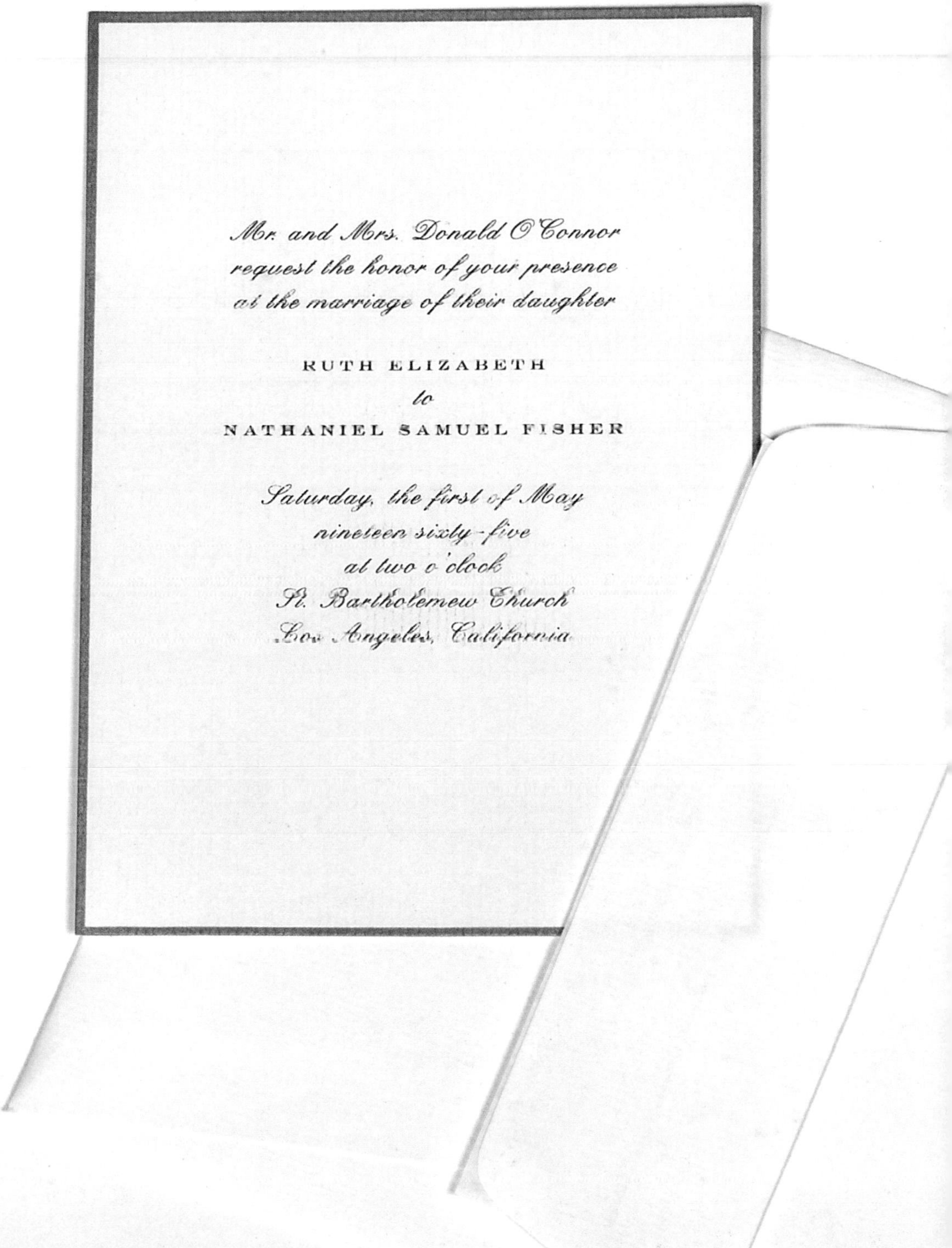

Mr. and Mrs. Donald O'Connor
request the honor of your presence
at the marriage of their daughter

RUTH ELIZABETH
to
NATHANIEL SAMUEL FISHER

Saturday, the first of May
nineteen sixty-five
at two o'clock
St. Bartholemew Church
Los Angeles, California

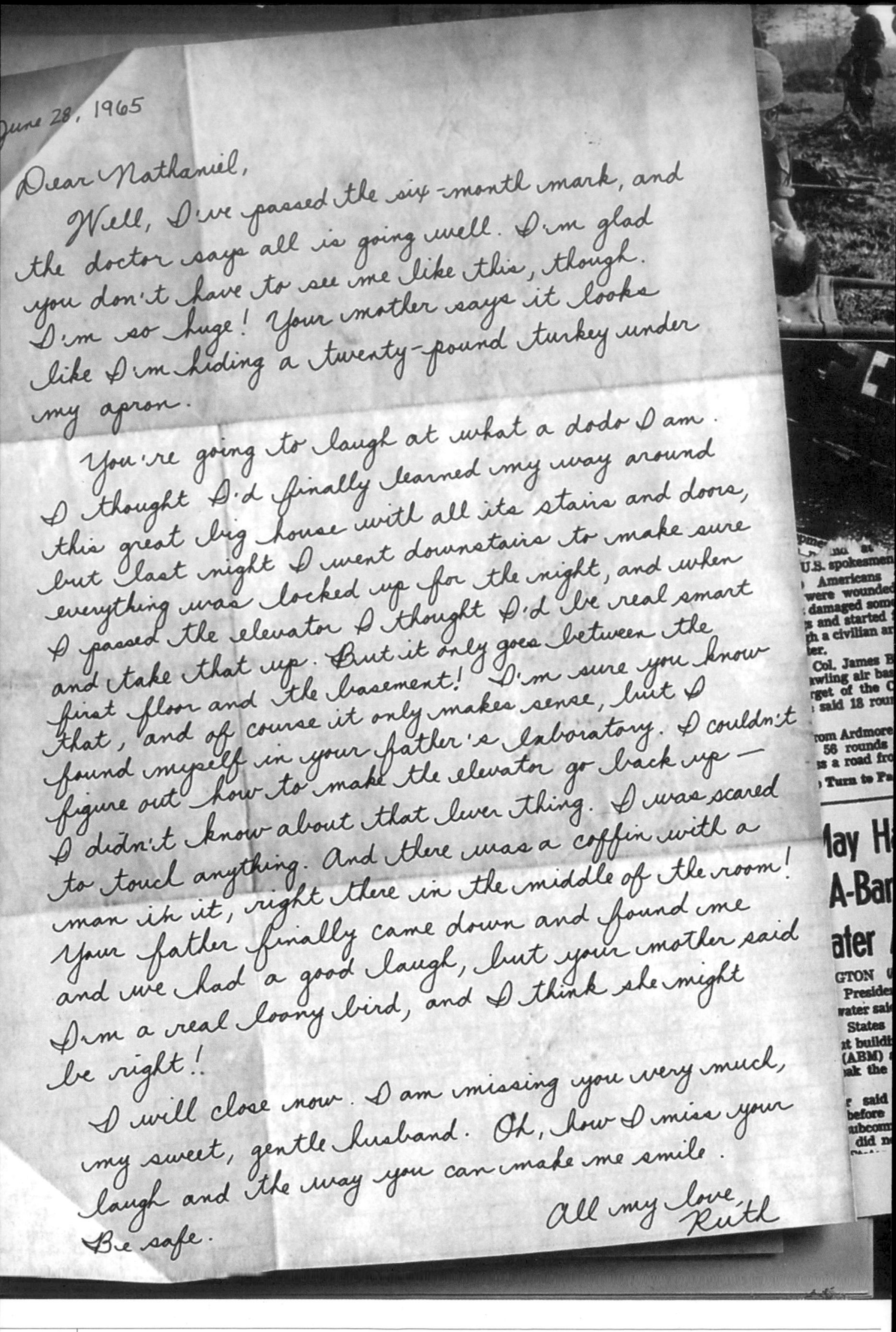

June 28, 1965

Dear Nathaniel,

Well, I've passed the six-month mark, and the doctor says all is going well. I'm glad you don't have to see me like this, though. I'm so huge! Your mother says it looks like I'm hiding a twenty-pound turkey under my apron.

You're going to laugh at what a dodo I am. I thought I'd finally learned my way around this great big house with all its stairs and doors, but last night I went downstairs to make sure everything was locked up for the night, and when I passed the elevator I thought I'd be real smart and take that up. But it only goes between the first floor and the basement! I'm sure you know that, and of course it only makes sense, but I found myself in your father's laboratory. I couldn't figure out how to make the elevator go back up — I didn't know about that lever thing. I was scared to touch anything. And there was a coffin with a man in it, right there in the middle of the room! Your father finally came down and found me and we had a good laugh, but your mother said I'm a real loony bird, and I think she might be right!.

I will close now. I am missing you very much, my sweet, gentle husband. Oh, how I miss your laugh and the way you can make me smile. Be safe.

All my love
Ruth

DEAREST RUTH,   DECEMBER 25, 1965

THIS SURE ISN'T LIKE ANY WAR I'VE EVER HEARD OF.
YESTERDAY I WAS HUNKERING DOWN IN QUE SON, TRYING
NOT TO GET MY BIG EARS SHOT OFF, PATCHING UP OUR
BOYS AS FAST AS I COULD, AND TODAY I SAT OUT IN
THE SUN, WITH A COLD BEER IN MY HAND, A BELLYFUL
OF TURKEY AND GIBLETS. CHRISTMAS IN VIETNAM! I'D
TRADE IT ALL IN A SECOND TO BE AT HOME IN FRONT OF
THE FIREPLACE HOLDING YOU.

BUT DON'T YOU WORRY ABOUT ME. THAT MEDIC BADGE
I WEAR MAKES ME BULLETPROOF. I SURE DO MISS YOU,
THOUGH. HOPE YOU GOT THE LITTLE THINGS I SENT. AND
TELL LITTLE NATE THAT TEDDY BEAR IS ALL THE WAY
FROM VIETNAM!

WORD IS THAT OL' LBJ'S SENDING IN LOTS MORE
TROOPS, WHICH SHOULD PUT AN END TO THIS LITTLE BROUHAHA
PRETTY SOON. DON'T BE SURPRISED IF I'M HOME BY EASTER,
CARRYING A BASKET OF EGGS AND A CHOCOLATE BUNNY FOR
OUR BOY. I'LL POLISH UP THE CHEVY AND THE THREE OF US
WILL HEAD UP TO MALIBU FOR A PICNIC ON THE BEACH.

THIS ONE'S GOING TO BE SHORT — I'M AWFULLY TIRED.
SURE WISH YOU WERE HERE NEXT TO ME, DARLING.

     YOUR KNIGHT IN SLIGHTLY RUSTED ARMOR,

       NATHANIEL

July 2, 1966

Dear Nathaniel,

I may be crazy, but I think Nathaniel Junior said his first sentence today. He looked up at me with those sweet eyes of his and clear as a bell said, "Where's Dada?" He was asking for you! He wanted to know when you're coming home. Maybe he was reading my mind.

He's such a good boy, but a rambunctious one at that. He's crawling faster than I can keep up. He climbed up onto our kitchen table today while I wasn't looking and took a tumble right onto his head. He cried and hollered, but as soon as he calmed down he was right back on that table. I spanked his little bottom, but I'm afraid that's not going to stop this one. I suppose I should expect nothing less from a son of yours. Your mother showed me a dent in the staircase where she said you tumbled all the way down when you were little. A good thing the Fisher boys have hard heads!

All my love,

Ruth

1966 | DURING NATHANIEL'S TOUR OF DUTY, HE AND RUTH WRITE EACH OTHER REGULARLY.

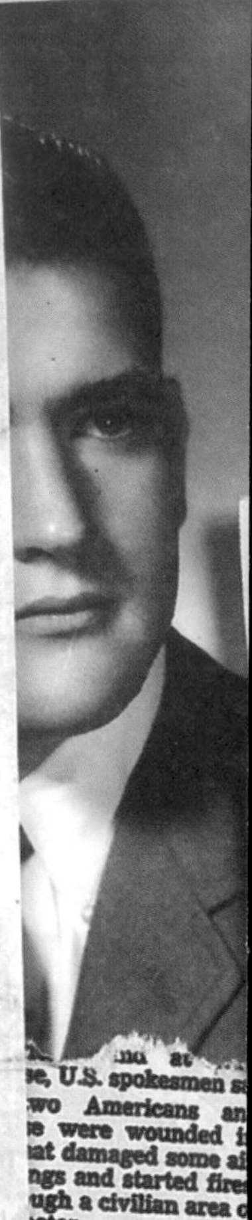

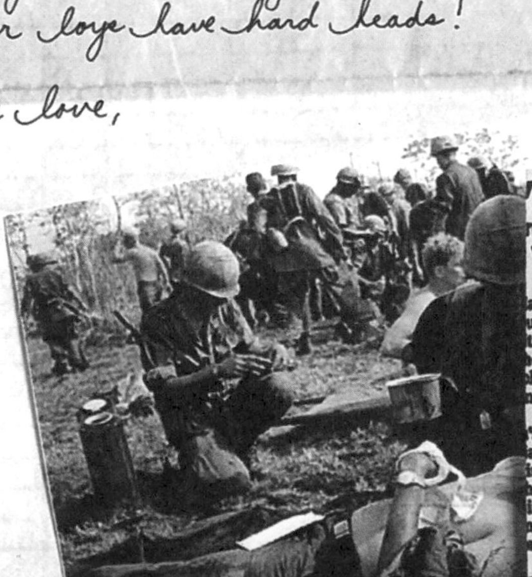

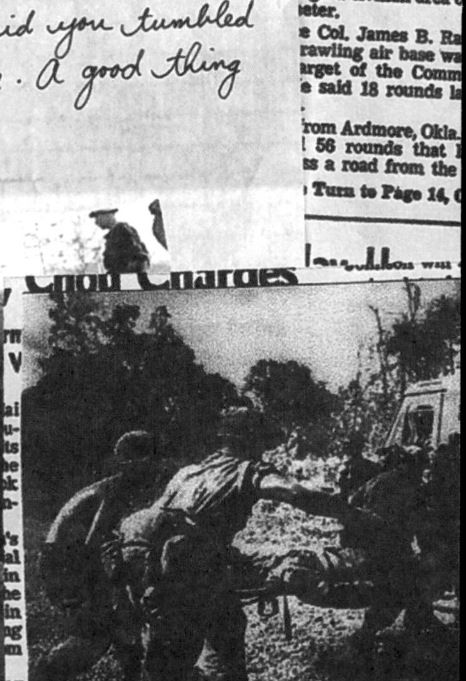

Dearest Ruth,

Keep those pictures coming. Good Lord, that's a handsome boy we got there! I have little Nate's pictures hanging right over my desk. You heard right, I've got a desk. You'll be happy to know I'm not "humping the boonies" anymore. Some wiseacre finally took a look at my records and saw my degree in mortuary science, so now I'm sitting pretty in Tan Son Nhut Air Base. I'm toiling away in the mortuary, the fighting miles away. The greatest danger to my health is falling into the latrine when I step out at night for a smoke. Got to say I feel guilty about this, leaving the rest of the boys back there, but you know I feel this is an important job, too. And it's a heckuva lot safer, so you and Nate can sleep a little more soundly.

Sometimes it almost feels like I'm back home. When I finish work, my clothes still smell of embalming fluid, and my shoulders are still in sore need of a good massage. But I suppose that's where it ends. The bodies they send me are all those of young men my own age, and most important of all, you're not there to greet me with a kiss at the top of the stairs when the work is done.

Give my little buddy boy a kiss from his Pop, and give yourself one, too.

Your loving husband,

Nathaniel

1964 | EUREKA'S SIDE-SERVICING LANDAU BOASTS AN ORNATE CASKET TABLE AND RICHLY APPOINTED INTERIOR.

What makes this hard on me is that I know
My parents-in-law think I seduced their so
overheard my husband's mother calling me
sure if our baby looks like her son. I had r
husband, and we were swept up in a mom
notice earlier in the day, and our favorite
trapped in a cage. I know it's horrible, but I f
at night, sometimes I take an extra second to
ents-in-law run a funeral home, which is w
being in the presence of so much death. Be

OCTOBER 6, 1966

DEAR PHYLLIS

Flummoxed In Funeral Home

DEAR PHYLLIS:

I am only 19 years old and a new mother. I have a beautiful baby boy. His father, my husband, is serving in Vietnam as a medic, and I'm living with my husband's parents. What makes this hard on me is that I know his parents think I got pregnant on purpose. My parents-in-law think I seduced their son and trapped him with our baby. I actually overheard my husband's mother calling me a floozy on the phone. She even said she's not sure if our baby looks like her son. I had never had an intimate relationship before my husband, and we were swept up in a moment of passion. He had just received his draft notice earlier in the day, and our favorite song came on the radio. Now I feel like I'm trapped in a cage. I know it's horrible, but I feel like my baby boy is the jailer. When he cries at night, sometimes I take an extra second to get out of bed. To make things worse, my parents-in-law run a funeral home, which is where we live, and I worry about my baby boy being in the presence of so much death. Because my husband's in Vietnam, I don't want to worry him. He is serving our country, so I don't tell him my real feelings. What should I do? Tell my husband the truth, or keep lying?

Sincerely,
At the End of My Rope

DEAR ROPE:
First things first: Did you get pregnant on purpose? Being honest with yourself and taking responsibility for your actions are two great ways to start addressing any problem.

Also, the first months of motherhood are always hard, but waiting to respond when a baby cries is a dangerous habit to cultivate. What if your baby is actually sick, or caught between the bars of your crib and unable to extricate himself? What if an animal such as a raccoon or possum has crawled in through an open window and is attacking your baby? (I only bring this up because of last week's letter from "Not To Blame.") When you hear that baby cry, you should rush in and see what's the matter, pronto!

As for living in a funeral home, I can imagine that takes a toll on you and makes it hard to deal with all of these formidable challenges. We all know death is a part of life, but being around actual dead bodies all the time makes for a morbid and depressive outlook. For your own well-being as well as your son's, I would set aside a little money and move out of there, and fast!

I think you should sit down with your mother-in-law and discuss all of these concerns honestly and openly with her. And do continue to write words of hope and encouragement to your husband in Vietnam: our fighting boys need all the support we can give them during this difficult time.

Yours,
Phyllis

is parents think I got pregnant on purpose
and trapped him with our baby. I actually
floozy on the phone. She even said she's not
ver had an intimate relationship before my
t of passion. He had just received his draf
ong came on the radio. Now I feel like I'm
l like my baby boy is the jailer. When he cries
et out of bed. To make things worse, my par-
ere we live, and I worry about my baby boy
use my husband's in Vietnam, I don't want

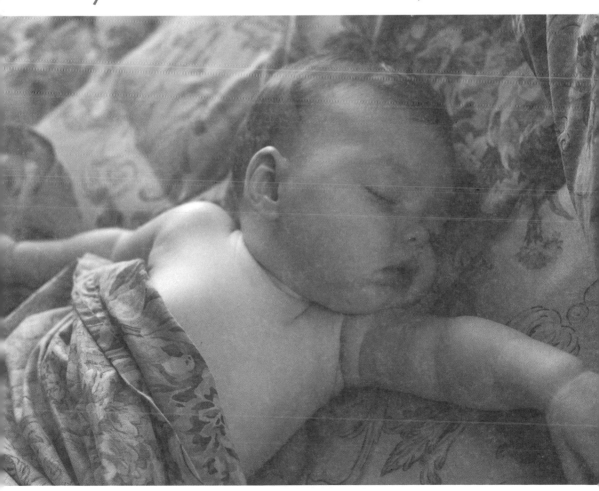

ECCLESIASTES 6:12

FOR WHO CAN KNOW WHAT IS GOOD FOR
A MAN IN HIS LIFE, THIS BRIEF SPAN
OF EMPTY EXISTENCE THROUGH WHICH
HE PASSES LIKE A SHADOW? WHO CAN
TELL A MAN WHAT IS TO HAPPEN NEXT
UNDER THE SUN?

How to create an illusion of vitality

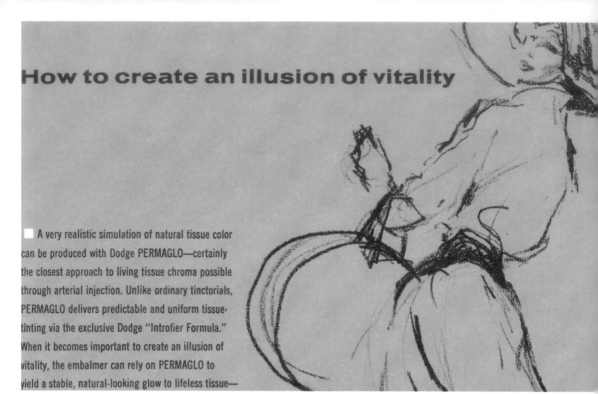

A very realistic simulation of natural tissue color can be produced with Dodge PERMAGLO—certainly the closest approach to living tissue chroma possible through arterial injection. Unlike ordinary tinctorials, PERMAGLO delivers predictable and uniform tissue-tinting via the exclusive Dodge "Introfier Formula." When it becomes important to create an illusion of vitality, the embalmer can rely on PERMAGLO to yield a stable, natural-looking glow to lifeless tissue—

Easy on the embalmer!

HALTS BAC

Dodge MYLO FIX NON-FUMING CAVITY CHEMICAL 16 FL. OZ.

MY

FOR FU

HIGH POTENCY W

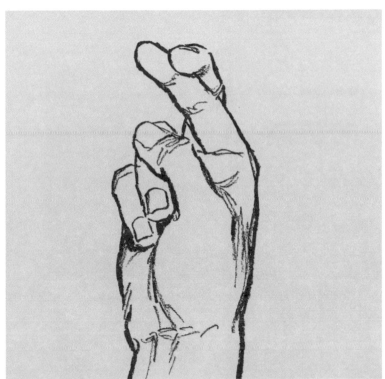

RIAL GROWTH!

LO-FIX

SENSITIVE EMBALMERS

AXIMUM WORKING COMFO

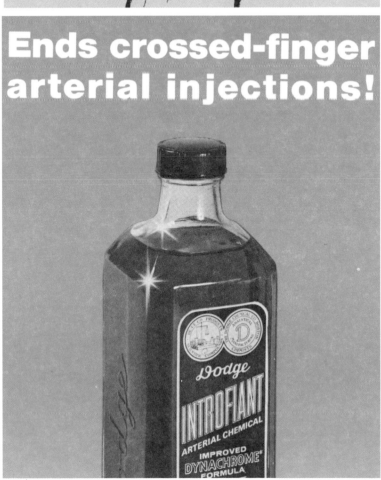

Ends crossed-finger arterial injections!

DEAR FELLOW MEMBERS
OF THE LOS ANGELES COMMUNITY,

I know it's unusual to address people personally in this type of advertisement, but that's exactly the point. Fisher & Sons Funeral Home has recently changed hands with the unfortunate passing of my father, Alfred Fisher. So while Fisher & Sons will continue to provide you with the same excellent level of quality mortuary services you have come to expect from us, we will also be adding a more personal touch to our business, which has been in my family since 1941. That is to say that I, Nathaniel Fisher, will now be dealing with clients personally. And furthermore, we would like you to consider us as members of your extended family. As a result, I personally promise to do everything within my power to help you find as much peace as possible with the passing of your loved ones, by providing them with the most dignified and loving service we can. Because, after all, our home is truly your home.

Sincerely,

NATHANIEL FISHER

Fisher & Sons
FUNERAL HOME

Dear Friends and Family,

1968 has been a year of big changes for the Fishers. Nathaniel's been home for a little over a year now, after nobly serving his country in Vietnam. He's almost completely readjusted to family life and work, although the continuous stream of bodies still being sent home from overseas does sometimes take a toll on him. I try to help the only way I know how, by being supportive and giving his back an encouraging rub every now and then. We are all so happy to have him home safe and with us again!

Little Nate turned three this year. He loves his Tinkertoys and his Lincoln Logs and is growing so fast! There is a little girl down the block named Shelby and he plays with her almost every day. They hold hands when they walk down the sidewalk together on the way to the park. It's so precious. They play a game called "Dig!" which I have not been able to figure out the rules for, but it seems to have something to do with finding pennies.

Make no mistake, though, Nate can also be a terror when he's in the mood. His favorite way to sass us is to say, "Forget what you said." He's so cute when he says it, I almost have to smile. That's when I thank my lucky stars I have Nathaniel to help me lay down the law. Also,

Nate's favorite foods right now are chocolate pudding, and sliced cucumbers with lemon juice. Quite a combination!

I took courses this year in a variety of topics: decoupage, crocheting, and leather tooling, to name a few, and for better or worse, the house is now filled with my handiwork. Santa might be bringing some of you very special presents this year, with real "homemade" style, so look out!

I also built my own crystal radio, with a little help from Nathaniel.

More good news: we are expecting another little baby in about six months! I think it is a girl, but Nathaniel is sure it's a boy. (It's a girl!)

On a sad note, Great Aunt Rose died this year. We had her service here at Fisher & Sons and everyone came from all over the country. She will be missed. But it was good to have Linda's Burnt Sugar Cake after so many years. How does she do that?

Well, what a big year! We hope your Christmas season is full of Christ's love.

Merry Christmas from Nathaniel, Ruth, Nate, and Baby On The Way

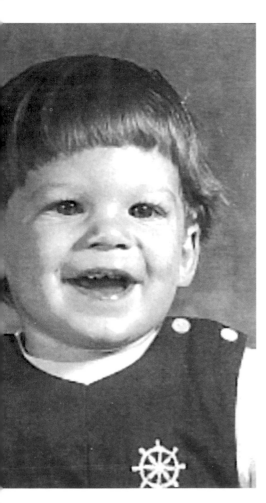

1969 | RUTH AND NATHANIEL HAVE THEIR SECOND CHILD, DAVID.

There was a time when there was lots of happiness.
When the boys were young. ~ RUTH

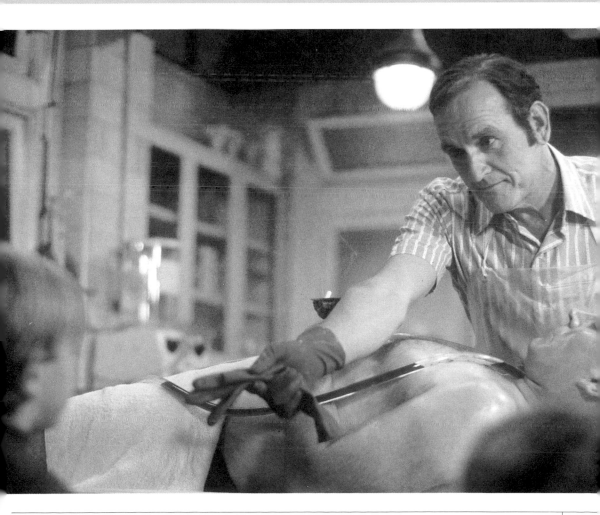

Dear Mr. Fisher,

I am writing to tell how much my brother H. and I are
thankful for you burying our mother and why we are so
late in finishing up business with you in terms of
paying our bill.

Our Mother was the only income wage-earner in our
family since our Father died. H. and I always did
our best to help out around the house, but for health
reasons like you must have "picked up on" when we met,
it is hard for us to work in the public sector, or to
even get jobs at all.

With Mother gone now, the landlord and other collectors
have "smelled the rat" and are showing up every day
asking what our plans are. H. is suffering badly from
the condition right now--it gets "angry" (Mother's
word) when times are hard, so that makes life at the
house even harder than usual. And I am in love with
a girl who doesn't know I exist, which is not a money
problem but does make it hard for me to concentrate.
Our disorder is not just a skin disorder; it makes
us very lonely. And of course I can never leave my
brother. Who am I kidding? Love is not possible for me.

We are so grateful for your kindness. We will pay you
when we can, promise.

Truly,

J. Umstead

J. Umstead

Dear Mr. Umstead,

Life can get enormously complicated after the death of a
loved one. I completely understand. Please put Fisher
& Sons at the bottom of your list of bills to pay
and know that we're always here for you should the need
for our services arise in the future.

Or perhaps, with all due respect, I can offer you an
unorthodox but helpful alternative to cash payment?

After your Mother's memorial service, your brother and I
had a long talk about something called "The Urantia Book."
Does this ring a bell? Is this something you're into as
well, or just your brother? I am not a follower of any
religion and never will be (might as well be up front
with you) but I've been looking for a copy of that thing
for years, ever since I heard about it from a buddy of
mine in the Army. He told me it's all about universes and
superuniverses and angels and how the Earth was formed…is
this the same book H. was talking about? If it is, and if
you wanted to, you two could send me a copy of that book
and we could call it even.

I spent a lot of long nights in the jungle listening to
my buddy talk about that book. I'd stare up at the stars
peeking through the trees, and he'd tell me all about
the life-carriers and superunivorses. It sounded pretty
amazing. Of course, he got killed, and that was the last
I heard anyone talk about the superuniverse. Until I met
you and your brother.

Anyway, what's most important is that you and your brother
are able to recover emotionally from the recent tragic
loss of your mother. That's my main concern. I'm not
waiting for you to pay me. That's not why I do what I do.

Sincerely,

Nathaniel Fisher

P.S. Don't give up on love, Mr. Umstead. Life can
surprise you when you least expect it.

1972 | AT AGE 7, NATE RECEIVES THE MOST VALENTINES OF ANY BOY IN HIS CLASS.

Nathaniel
and
Isabel

by j d wintour

illustrated by erica siskind

CHAPTER 5

The Perilous Bed

The rain had been falling in sheets all night. It was now three in the morning and the water in the cellar was ankle deep and getting deeper all the time. The distant sound of Nurse Caterwaul's terrible harpsichord playing and the oafish, appreciative grunts of her suitor, Mister Favisham, had been drifting down through the orphanage's ancient plumbing for hours, but suddenly the nightmarish music ceased and everything was silent. Nathaniel shivered. Isabel held him close and tried her best to comfort him.

"Surely Mother and Father will come to retrieve us soon?" Nathaniel asked. Nathaniel still believed that Mr. and Mrs. Davies would be returning from Norwich any day now. He still believed that their stay at Nurse Caterwaul's Blessed Home For Wayward Youths was temporary. Only Isabel knew the truth.

Suddenly the door at the top of the stairs flew open and the shadow of Nurse Caterwaul stretched down the staircase. Her sour voice shrieked, "Children!"

"Yes, Nurse Caterwaul," Isabel responded from the darkness in a supremely reasonable tone, as though she were speaking from behind a don's desk at Oxford, and not from the bottom of what was essentially a torture chamber.

"Mister Favisham has asked if he might join me for tea," Nurse Caterwaul said. Her voice was so thick with drink and tipsy-topsy-turvy that listening to it almost made Nathaniel and Isabel seasick.

"The ever-so naughty Mister Favisham has indicated an interest in my poetry," Nurse Caterwaul said in her sing-song tone. "He thinks I have sensitivity." But then something mysterious and obviously obscenely hilarious happened which prevented Nurse Caterwaul from continuing. She hooted like a fat old owl.

Suddenly the voice of Mister Favisham grunted, "We'll be in the attic!"

"So don't bother screaming!" cackled Caterwaul.

"We can't hear you!" croaked Favisham, his voice trailing away.

"Sweet dreams!" Nurse Caterwaul wailed.

And the cellar door slammed shut. Huddled together on the bed, Nathaniel and Isabel gazed around the cellar, trying to re-adjust their eyes once more to the pitch-black darkness. The rain outside continued to crash down like a thousand trains full of screaming commercial travelers being smashed and smashed and smashed.

"The water certainly seems to be rising ever more rapidly," Nathaniel chattered. He was right. Many small bottles of Nurse Caterwaul's patented laxative tonics were now floating aimlessly around the cellar like haunted little boats on a poisoned sea, along with several ragged sheets of waterlogged paper and one dead rat. "I d-d-d-don't want to drown," said Nathaniel.

"We won't drown, Nathaniel. Don't worry."

But just then the tiny bed—upon which Isabel had spent many nights being lectured, whipped, and, sometimes, "irrigated" by Nurse Caterwaul (there were a lot of things Isabel never told Nathaniel because they would only frighten him unnecessarily) —just then the bed began to float across the cellar. From the far corner came the sound of ancient stone, wetly cracking and crumbling.

"What's happening, Isabel?" asked Nathaniel, panicking. "What's happening to us?"

The crashing of the rain outside suddenly seemed louder than before.

"If I'm not mistaken, Nathaniel, we're about to be . . . how shall I put this?" Isabel had an unquenchable passion for finding the right word—"le mot juste," as her favorite writer, Mr. Flaubert, used to say.

"Killed?" offered Nathaniel.

1975 | AN EXCERPT FROM CHAPTER FIVE OF *NATHANIEL AND ISABEL*, THE FIRST BOOK IN THE SERIES.

"No, not killed."

A hole the size of a sea dragon's mouth suddenly opened in the far corner of the cellar and the disgusting water began roaring and rushing out into the night. Nathaniel screamed another verbal option over his shoulder at Isabel as the bed shot across the floor like a schooner.

"Pulverized?"

"No, not exactly pulverized," judged Isabel, still as calm as ever.

And now the wall of crushing rain and the vast valley that lay beneath the promontory upon which the orphanage stood yawned before Nathaniel and Isabel as they careered through the ever widening hole in the orphanage cellar wall and Isabel finally found the word for which she'd been searching.

"Delivered!"

And with that, the two adventurers, astride that perilous bed, which for months had been the source of such unspeakable misery to poor Isabel, rode the newborn river (still dotted with laxative tonics and, now, dozens of quite live rats), they rode it up and up and—CRASH!—over the edge of the cliff and sailed directly into the eye of the raging storm.

Nathaniel swooned and lost consciousness.

Isabel 1) made a mental note to tell Nathaniel the truth about their parents once they were safe and dry (both dead, Norwich Silk Works, terrible fire, couldn't be helped); 2) made another mental note to reread Flaubert's *Sentimental Education* ("It's such a superb piece of prose," she thought to herself, fleetingly); and then, business taken care of, she 3) screamed bloody murder in the face of certain death, just like the terrified little girl she truly was.

• • •

THE PERILOUS BED   25

"And the thought of all those helpless silkworms perishing in the fire was more than Mother and Father could bear," said Isabel. "They rushed back in to save them, just as the building collapsed."

"They died to save silkworms?" said Nathaniel, snuffling through his tears. "Little helpless silkworms?"

"Yes. You know Mother and Father held all life to be holy and worthy of respect." And indeed, it was true. For an immensely rich and sophisticated couple, the Davies had always maintained a keen interest in all sorts of esoteric philosophies and charitable works. Mrs. Davies had always fashioned herself a Buddhist. Mr. Davies had preferred to think of himself simply as someone with "a good heart, trying his best."

"May I have another crumpet with jam?" asked Nathaniel sweetly. They were the only children seated in the shiny sunlit dining room of the Southwold Hotel. In fact, they were the only people seated there at all. The sweet old waiter, Huntz, the same Huntz who'd been so much help at the carnival the night before, was standing only a few yards away, staring through the windows out towards the grey sea.

"Of course, Nathaniel, you can have all the crumpets you want. All the crumpets you want." Isabel elegantly raised her index finger in the waiter's direction. "Huntz?"

Huntz approached the table with a look of great benevolence and unspeakable sadness. You'd never know from looking at this wrinkled old fellow that, when it became necessary, he was able to ride a stampeding elephant through a crowd of small children with such effortless élan.

"Yes, Mistress Isabel?"

"Another crumpet for my brother, please. And some fresh, hot Earl Grey for me, please. This cup's grown tepid, I'm afraid."

"Of course," said Huntz, and headed off for the kitchen.

Nathaniel looked out at the sea and wiped his nose with his napkin. He spoke in a tone that smacked of newfound strength.

"Mother and Father would have liked it here."

"Yes," Isabel concurred. "They would have liked it here very much."

She set her hand gently on his and wrinkled her nose, trying not to cry.

CHAPTER 12

1975 | AN EXCERPT FROM CHAPTER TWELVE OF *NATHANIEL AND ISABEL*.

And as they sat there, an angelic silence slowly settled over Nathaniel and Isabel. The peaceful quiet of the dining room, broken only by the soft sound of a teacup clinking on a saucer somewhere. The grey-pink morning light reflecting off the waves. The sense of having come to the end of a long and painful journey. It all combined to fill both of the children with a feeling of security and safety more rich and deep than anything they had ever felt before.

They didn't know Nurse Caterwaul was on the third floor of the Southwold Hotel at that very moment, growling and smiling tightly while Mister Favisham and the manager kicked down the door to Room 37 in search of the missing Davies children. They didn't know that in a matter of months they'd be prisoners of The Blue Devil on a scurvy pirate ship off the Barbary Coast. They didn't know they'd be sold as slaves in the Belgian Congo and forced to eat live maggots and monkey flesh, which the natives called "bush meat." They didn't know they'd be running from Nurse Caterwaul for the rest of their lives.

At that moment, Huntz returned with Nathaniel's crumpet and Isabel's tea and set them down on the table. The steam rose from the delicate white teacup like a little dream, slowly dissolving.

• • •

Hello Janet,

If there's an emergency of any sort, dial 9-1-1. All the contact phone numbers are on the cabinet over the sink. The boys can play with their Lincoln Logs or any of the games in the toy chest in the sun porch. Don't let them talk you into going outside to ride bikes in the driveway. For dinner, you can make Nate a ham or turkey sandwich, whichever he prefers. I left the ingredients on the counter, except the meat, which is in the "Meats" drawer in the refrigerator. He can have milk to drink—no soda. For dessert, he can have fruit or a popsicle. David might eat some ham if you cut it up into strips. If he doesn't want ham, try turkey. Absolutely no mustard or condiments of any kind. He drinks his milk at room temperature and won't want any dessert. Their bedtime is 7:30 P.M. Their pajamas are folded on each of their beds. Don't let David talk you into wearing a different set. Please watch to make sure they brush their teeth for at least two minutes. They each like a story before bed. Let them choose one from the shelf next to Nate's bed. Please keep the night light on in David's room and the hall light on, with Nate's door open a crack. He'll show you how wide open he likes it. We'll be home by 10:30.

~ Ruth

Adams Street Elementary School	Year-End Report Card		
NAME: David Fisher	GRADE: 1	DATE: June 7, 1976	TEACHER: Miss Reid

SUBJECT	GRADE	COMMENTS
Math	A-	Great improvement
Science	B+	Good work
Art	A	Excellent work
Music	A	Lots of talent!!!!
Reading	A-	Great improvement
Writing	A-	Good work
Physical Education	C-	Needs improvement

Notes:
David remains a bright, friendly child who listens well and gets along with the other students. He has shown great improvement in his Math and Reading Comprehension skills over the course of the year. He struggled a bit with his weekly spelling quizzes and getting his Science assignments completed on time. He also seemed to have difficulty concentrating in Gym Class; the teacher had to pull him aside several times for spending more time socializing with the other boys than learning the rules of play. Overall, it was a very positive experience teaching your son and I wish him much luck in the 2nd grade.

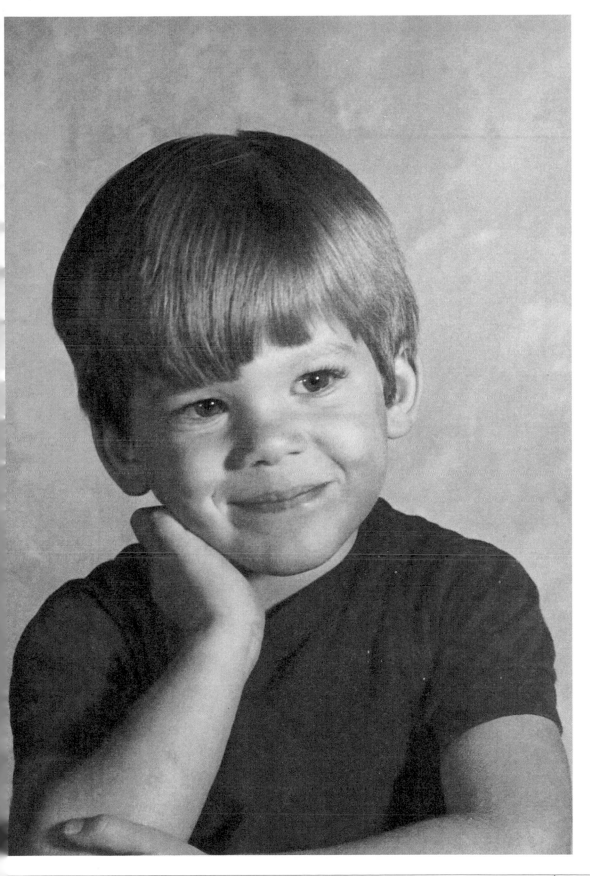

THE TIBETAN BOOK OF LIVING AND DYING

WE ASSUME, STUBBORNLY AND
UNQUESTIONINGLY, THAT PERMANENCE
PROVIDES SECURITY AND IMPERMA-
NENCE DOES NOT. BUT, IN FACT,
IMPERMANENCE IS LIKE SOME OF THE
PEOPLE WE MEET IN LIFE—
DIFFICULT AND DISTURBING AT FIRST,
BUT ON DEEPER ACQUAINTANCE
FAR FRIENDLIER AND LESS UNNERVING
THAN WE COULD HAVE IMAGINED.

But I Never Made Funeral Arrangements Before!

Should The Body Be Present At The Funeral

WITH THE BODY PRESENT

Why Do We H
Funerals,
Anyway?

ould I Go
The Funeral?
t Do I Say?

Contemplate It
By Brenda Chenowith, Age 8 ½

You can stare at it.

You can pet it.

You can ignore it.

You can put it

on a bed of fluffy golden pillows

and worship it.

You can try to stump it.

You can put other things beside it

and draw comparisons.

That's all you can do.

My Balloons
By Brenda Chenowith, Age 8

My heart is blowing balloons up

because I am happy.

The little balloons go sailing up through my arteries

and into my brain.

It's like a park in there,

where people have picnics

and sailboats on the lake.

And there are little red balloons everywhere,

popping and popping

on the thorny, thorny branches of the trees.

The Handsome Prince

By Brenda Chenowith, Age 10

The prince was so handsome.

he was like a prison girls had to escape from.

Many tried.

And none succeeded.

Until there came to the Red Kingdom an enchanted girl named Christina.

When she marched across the little footbridge to greet the prince.

everyone could tell by the look on her face

it was going to be a regular war of kissing.

Soon they were face to face in their private room.

Even the old. dusty books on the shelf were wondering what would happen next.

The handsome prince gazed into the eyes of the enchanted girl

and tried to lock her up in the dungeon of his gaze.

But she escaped.

And this is how she did it:

In the corner of his gaze there was a rope.

and she climbed it. up through a hole in the ceiling.

into a secret chamber.

No one had ever been there. The dust was as thick as pancakes on the floor

with nary a footprint.

And the secret chamber was full of smelly old cardboard boxes. all marked "secret."

So the enchanted girl made a flame with her fingers.

set fire to all the secrets, and got out of there fast.

stopping only to save a little kitten that had been hiding in the corner.

The prince never even knew what had happened to him.

His handsomeness was nothing to him now.

He was heartbroken and he didn't know why.

He would miss the enchanted girl forever.

Charlotte
Light and Dark
by Gareth Feinberg Ph.D.

MEDICAL

MENTAL HEALTH

SELF HELP

UCLA

1976 | BRENDA CHENOWITH, BRILLIANT BUT UNCONTROLLABLE, IS SENT TO PSYCHOLOGIST GARETH FEINBERG, PH.D.

DR. FEINBERG TURNS HIS EXTENSIVE STUDY OF BRENDA INTO A BESTSELLER CALLED *CHARLOTTE LIGHT AND DARK*.

7

The Swarming Indifference

It was January now. Many of my colleagues had chosen to spend their winter break on holiday in Mexico or the Caribbean, but I had remained in the chilly network of San Francisco's fogbound streets. I was fearful that without continued treatment Charlotte would slip into genuine madness. It was a desperate time.

For several months, Charlotte and I had been meeting in my office on the San Francisco State campus twice a week: Thursdays, after school, and Saturday mornings. We spent these sessions playing chess (she invariably beat me in less than twenty moves); talking about books (she'd just finished *Atlas Shrugged* and judged it "kinda pointless for such a big fat book"); or, occasionally, she would spend the entire session sitting across from me, mirroring my every move, while humming the themes from her favorite cartoons.

One day I arrived for our scheduled session a little late and found Charlotte seated at my desk, trying her best to look authoritative with my pipe in her mouth. She had been reading a memo about my work at Hempstead Hospital, a residential facility in nearby Palo Alto. She asked if she could spend a few weeks there.

"Why would you want go to Hempstead?" I asked. "It's a mental hospital."

"I know," she replied, dropping the memo into the wastebasket. "It would be like summer camp." She narrowed her eyes and smiled. "Maybe you could even stage a panty raid, Doctor Fatburg. You could try to kiss me and then I could throw up all over your big, fat face. Like this." She began to gag herself with my pipe. I bounded across the room and forcibly removed the pipe from her hand, and her from my chair.

After I placed her on the couch, she sat there flouncily and glared at me.

"If you ever touch me again," she said, "my brother's gonna eat your weiner."

It was a typical Charlotte moment.

Nevertheless, with her parents' permission, arrangements were indeed soon made for Charlotte to spend three weeks in January at Hempstead for "observation." Plans were made to administer various psychological inventories, in order to give the whole experience the ring of truth. Actually, though, I was hoping that time spent in the company of the truly troubled might shock the ever dissimulating Charlotte into sincerity.

After a few days at Hempstead, Charlotte struck up a friendship with Stephen, another young patient of mine. They were both the only children on locked Ward E (Charlotte, at 7, was one year Stephen's senior) and thus naturally gravitated to each other. Stephen had been placed under my care after a failed suicide attempt that left his arms slashed to ribbons. I was anxious for him to establish a positive connection with someone, so I sanctioned the budding friendship. Like Charlotte, Stephen was intensely intelligent and an avid reader, so the two of them got along quite well. They spent endless hours playing a complicated word game they called "Vagina Brittania," the rules of which neither myself nor my staff were ever able to fathom. It seemed to have something to do with linking obscure quotations from literature with infantile metaphors for masturbation. There was also some basic algebra involved. I felt that as long as their friendship was never allowed to become physical, this kind of "naughty" talk could be allowed, could even be therapeutic. Perhaps I was mistaken.

For soon, Charlotte and Stephen were spending virtually all their free time together. They ceased to take any part in group therapy. They both became increasingly reticent with me in private sessions. What had begun as a potentially healthy friendship was rapidly becoming an obsession. I resolved to separate the pair by moving Charlotte into Ward C. She greeted the suggestion with suspicion.

"Is that where you kill people?" she asked me.

"No," I countered. "Ward C is actually a much more pleasant environment than Ward E. Your room will look out on a garden. You'll have your own refrigerator."

"Can Stephen come too?"

"No, he needs to remain in Ward E for a few more weeks."

She scowled.

"You're only here for observation and testing, Charlotte. Stephen's here for more serious reasons."

"Then I'll stay in Ward E."

"Charlotte, it's not your choice." And then, as she did whenever she was confronted with limits of any kind, she began barking like a mad dog. I sat there and did my best to affect a look of implacable boredom. But this time her performance lasted several more minutes, becoming more and more passionate, until she was actually foaming at the mouth, pounding her tiny fists on the table. Her eyes were wild. The session had come to an end.

But the pine green and lavender bruises on her hands lasted for weeks.

* * *

Charlotte was moved out of Ward E. The actual move was uneventful by Charlotte's standards. The morning she was to be moved, she pretended to be sound asleep. A quartet of orderlies packed her things while she lay there, snoring theatrically, and then carried her limp body down the busy halls of the hospital. After we had deposited her in her new room and the orderlies had left, she finally opened her eyes and spoke, without moving, just as

I was walking out the door.

"You hate me," she said.

Surprised, I turned back. "No, Charlotte, I don't hate you. What a thing to say."

She stared at me blankly for a moment.

"This whole mental hospital is nothing but a giant lie—a lie so big it takes a thousand people to tell it." Now her face was starting to be expressive, to knot up with childlike resentment. "And you, Doctor Fartburg, are just one word, just one word in the world's biggest lie."

"And what," I asked, "is the world's biggest lie?"

I stood there in the doorway for a full minute, waiting for an answer. Finally, it came.

"That you're not in love with my mother."

Charlotte had hinted many times at the notion that I was her real father—and that my own self-hatred for deserting her is what had led me to study her in such painstaking detail. "The world's biggest lie, Doctor Fatburglar, is I'm not your precious little baby girl."

I walked out of the room and closed the door gently behind me. There was clearly no talking to her today.

* * *

The next morning, Stephen purposefully hammered several thick nails into his leg during Arts and Crafts and had to be rushed to the emergency room. When Charlotte heard about the incident, she came and found me in my office. As always, she burst in without knocking.

"Happy?" she shrieked at me. Her face was streaked with tears.

"Charlotte," I said, knowing exactly why she'd come, "the fact that Stephen responds to being separated from you this way is proof that the bond between you two is unhealthy."

"Can I go back to Ward E?" she asked plaintively.

"Positively not. You'll do better in Ward C, and truthfully, Charlotte, Stephen will be better off without you."

"You think you know what's best for everybody," she said.

"No, but I think I know in some cases what is best for some people. That's what being a doctor is all about."

"You're not a doctor. You're not even a person."

She wiped her nose on her shirtsleeve and straightened up, suddenly striking a tone that reeked of rehearsal.

"You're nothing but a swarming indifference, fit only to be politely disregarded." And like a princess flanked on either side by a quietly chattering coterie of gentlewomen, she spun regally round and left my office.

I was gradually coming to realize that neither Charlotte's passion for a friend such as Stephen, nor her feelings toward her immediate family, nor her anger towards me—none of these emotions would ever eclipse the basic level of pleasure she could generate through the construction of dramatic moments such as the one just described. Whenever I thought I'd found something Charlotte truly cared about, she would double back and surprise me with unimaginable callousness. When I thought she didn't care about something, she made a point of taking an inordinately passionate stand. Nothing, it seemed, was more important to her than holding the attention of everyone around her through the device of being continually, maddeningly surprising.

It was only several weeks later that I realized her parting shot at me had been lifted, in toto, from a novel by Thomas Hardy.

* * *

Stephen's parents elected, in the wake of his horrific self-mutilation, to move him to a different hospital. Charlotte seized upon this turn of events as the excuse for a host of ever more unsettling displays. The dynamic of dependence she traditionally perpetuated with her younger brother, Adam, had been transferred, while under my care, to Stephen—and without him to play his part in her psychological drama, Charlotte became divergent, playing both roles at once.

First, she stopped eating. After she had gone two days without food, I alerted her parents to the situation. Only when they threatened to visit did she relent.

Next came a period of false cooperativeness, during which Charlotte performed a battery of psychological tests, answering every question as facetiously as possible. A few sample responses from her Miller Analogies test provide a picture of her mental state during this time:

Apple is to seed as grown-up is to:

A) Baby   B) Grandma   C) Orange   D) Window

Charlotte chose none of the above, scribbling the name "Hitler" in the space provided. Or this:

Architect is to building as baker is to:

A) Bakery   B) Fortune   C) Limit   D) Cake

Charlotte's answer? "Doctor Finkburg's Poopy Buns."

The final test I administered involved Charlotte making up stories based on black-and-white photographs. While I knew the creative aspect of this exercise would appeal to Charlotte's playful side, I was also hoping that I'd be able to glimpse, through the free play of her imagination, the key to unlocking her spirit, that spirit bound up in the ever constricting net of an almost terminal self-consciousness.

Her narrative work with the pictures was initially encouraging. As I listened to Charlotte spin long, elegant tales from these often quite mundane images, I thought I sensed a naturalness that had been kept from me up until this very moment. But the story she told in response to the last image—that of a young farm girl and an old man standing in front of a grain elevator on the open prairie—showed me how wrong I'd been. I reproduce it below in full, transcribed word for word from the tape of our session.

Charlotte: "The little girl was coming out to the mailbox, because she is waiting for a letter from the Army. There is a war in Pennsylvania and her brother is fighting in it. He is a demolition paratrooper. He explodes when he lands on the ground. When he explodes, the Army will send a letter to the little girl with a treasure map about where to find her brother's heart on the battlefield when the war is over. So she is always going to the mailbox to check."

Me: "And who's the old man?"

Charlotte: "He's her doctor."

Me: "Is the little girl sick?"

Charlotte: "No."

Me: "Then why is the doctor there?"

Charlotte: "He's there because he took the picture."

(Silence.)

Me: "He took the picture, and he's in it at the same time?"

Charlotte: "Yes."

Me: "How did he do that?"

Charlotte: "He took it by hanging the camera on a hook stuck in a cloud. And then he made the little girl stand there while the picture took itself."

Me: "And why does the doctor want to take the picture?"

(Silence.)

Charlotte: "Because he doesn't know he exists if he isn't making someone do something. That's why he follows the girl everywhere. He's a shadow."

It was at this moment I realized that in my twenty years of practicing psychology, I'd never dealt with a psyche as stubborn and resistant as Charlotte's. Raised by a pair of successful analysts, immersed as she was in the culture of self-awareness, she had no way to stop watching herself, no possible avenue of escape from the jewel-like hall of mirrors that was her mind. I saw no hope for further progress and resolved to release her into the custody of her parents. The brief experiment had come to an end.

Or so I thought. For just then, Charlotte did the one thing I had come to believe she would never, ever do.

* * *

Dear Mr. and Mrs. Fisher,

In the past few months, Nathaniel has shown signs of behavior that may, over time, seriously distract him from academics and profoundly affect his future. I don't know quite how to put this. Frankly, he's gone girl-crazy. As Nate is already challenged in terms of concentration and focus on his studies, I feel strongly that we should nip this in the bud.

Boys and girls generally make tentative efforts toward verbal and physical interaction in junior high school. After 20 years of teaching, I am quite used to the gentle patterns of approach and retreat, the intricate and delicate social minuets that mark a child's passage into puberty. It can really be quite charming.

However, Nate seems to have bypassed this phase completely. In fact, I would go so far as to call him physically precocious. And his behavior affects the behavior of the girls. Classes are often disrupted by a veritable hailstorm of love notes flying at him from every corner of the room. Administrators, secretaries, teachers, teachers' aides, janitors and monitors regularly discover him and assorted girlfriends in flagrante delicto, making out in closets, under bleachers, in unoccupied class space, by lockers, in the gym, virtually everywhere on school grounds. He has even been found in possession of "make-out" maps.

In addition, he has been reprimanded several times for not only french-kissing but GRINDING in the halls.

I am sure you share my alarm and concern. Please call to make an appointment for another Parent/Teacher conference.

Sincerely,

Mrs. Antonia Carter
Guidance Counselor
Henry Francis Middle School

July 6, 1981

Dear Sarah,

I can't go to bed tonight without expressing how deeply angry I am with you. There is nothing in this world more precious to me than my two boys, and when I entrusted you with their care this weekend, I had every expectation that you would treat them with the same regard.

It's simply beyond my understanding how you could have let my Nate be molested by that woman. He's fifteen years old, for God's sake! He's a child. I can only imagine what kind of emotional scarring this might leave on him. He's closed up in his bedroom right now, and when I tried to comfort him, he'd have nothing to do with me. I can only think that this horrid experience has left him afraid of all women, and what a terrible thing to do to a boy!

As for little David, I can't even begin to fathom what kind of trauma he experienced while you were taking care of him. He was bleeding from the ear, his new summer trousers were filled with brambles, and there was so much filth under his fingernails I had to scour them for a good ten minutes. But what truly terrifies me is how much worse it could have been. Those hills are filled with coyotes and mountain lions. They could have made a feast of my young boy! Not to mention the vagabonds that skulk through those back roads. Have you no sense at all?

The only possible explanation for this kind of behavior on your part is that you are still taking drugs. I had sincerely hoped that you had grown out of that phase, or at least had the maturity to put them away for just one weekend. Was that so much to ask? It truly breaks my heart, but I can't possibly entrust the care of my children with you ever again.

Your sister,
Ruth

SANTA FE! CITY OF THE HOLY FAITH!
END OF THE SANTA FE TRAIL

Ruth—
Oh my lord, you must come to Santa Fe. It is simply beyond description how beautiful it is up in the mountains and the vibe is so cool and the people are all so real and i think I've truely found my home here in this little corner of the world. Come! Sarah

POST CARD

RUTH FISHER
2302 W. 25th St.
Los Angeles, CA.

Dear Mr. Dillon,

I just saw the movie Little Darlings and wanted to tell you that I really liked it a lot! You were really good and so was Kristy McNichol as Angel.

I liked the part when you were riding your motorcycle and Angel comes to see you. Did you already know how to do wheelies, or did someone teach you? My brother Nate said it wasn't you on the bike. He said you probably used a stunt double so you wouldn't get hurt. But I thought it looked like you were driving the whole time.

My brother wants to get a motorcycle like yours when he turns 16, but I don't think my dad will let him unless he uses a stunt double! My dad says people are always getting killed in motorcycle accidents. He knows because he's a funeral director and sees dead people all the time.

Was it hard learning your lines? Last year I played a mutinous sailor in my school play about Christopher Columbus. My line was "Turn back, Columbus!" but I kept forgetting where I was supposed to come in. I heard that some people have a photographic memory and can just look at a page and remember everything word for word. My mom says Henry Fonda can do that. He's going to be in that new movie with his daughter Jane Fonda. She's one of my mom's favorite actresses but I don't think she has a photographic memory. Do you know them?

Do you have any new movies coming out? I think they should make a sequel to Little Darlings but it should be about the boys side of camp, instead of the girls. I've never been to summer camp but me and my brother used to go to my Aunt Sarah's sometimes and camp out in her back yard with her and a bunch of her friends. My mom won't let us go anymore though because she thinks my Aunt Sarah is a bad influence and because I got lost in the canyon when she was supposed to be watching me.

Well, I guess I should be going. If you get a chance, can you send me an autographed picture? I have a wall in my room that I set aside for pictures. I have a picture of Nadia Comaneci from the Olympics! She signed it when we met her at Disneyland.

Thank you and have a nice day!

Sincerely,
David Fisher

Dear Ilya,

Zdrastvuitye! Thanks for writing me back! Those stamps you used were so COOL! I am soaking them to save for my collection. Thanks for your picture too. The one I'm sending is from last year because we haven't gotten our new ones from school yet. The reason I'm wearing a patch is because I scratched my eye the day before we took our pictures. I'll send you a new one when they come.

To answer your question, no I've never had blini before. Those sound good though! My favorite food is spaghetti and meatballs. My dad makes his own homemade sauce.

As for my favorite sport, I like bowling. Have you ever played? I just started playing with my church youth group and it's awesome! It's the only sport I've ever beaten my brother Nate in. He's 4 years older and will be graduating from high school in May. It's funny how our whole lives we've been in school together and after this year, Nate will be totally done and probably move out. It'll be weird not seeing him every day.

On top of that, my mom just told us she's pregnant and that I'll have a NEW brother or sister in March. I feel like everything is changing all of a sudden and there's nothing I can do about it. I know it's stupid, but sometimes I just wish things could stay the way they are. Do you ever think that?

Anyway, I guess I should get going. I still have a ton of Algebra homework to do (YUCK!).

TAKE CARE AND WRITE SOON! DUS VIDANIYA!

David

Dear Mr. and Mrs. Fisher,

As you can see from Nate's Life-Skills Inventory I've sent along, Nate is continuing to take his future less than seriously. I am not the only person at Bonaventure who is concerned about this. Many students with less intelligence than Nate have already secured spots at top colleges. Nate's failure to apply himself is all that stands between him and a good education and a good job. If you think that a conference at school with you both, myself, and Nate would serve to "shake him up" a little, then I am in total agreement. Nate is a young man with lots of natural charm and potential—I'd hate to see him spend the next four years the way he's spent the last three. Please give me a call at my office if you'd like to set up an appointment.

Fondly,

Anne Kordinak

Anne Kordinak

P.S. The parents of Evangeline Feier have made their peace with the situation that arose between Vangie and Nate during the fall semester, so I think we can all breathe a sigh of relief and put it behind us. At our last meeting, I mentioned it in passing to Nate, and he, too, seemed to feel it had blown over. This, at least, is good news.

LIFE-SKILLS INVENTORY

Nate Fisher, Grade 12

WHAT DO YOU WANT TO BE?

I want to be an astronaut, because then I could live on the moon. On the moon, there are lunar modules with sound systems that kick ass. This is one great reason to live on the moon, in addition to the fact that weightlessness—anti-gravity—would make it easy to hop over anything that gets in your way. Also, the telephones work different there, and there is no S.A.T.! (Ha!) Seriously, I do not want to be a businessman, but maybe the manager of a rock band or a guitarist in one like Boomtown Rats or the E Street Band. (Springsteen's backup band! The Boss rules!) This is maybe not as realistic as it seems, but neither is this test.

Two things I will NEVER be are

1) mortician/funeral director and

2) married!

Because both of those things are unnatural and anti-life, which is another advantage to the moon-based life I was advocating. The sound system in the lunar module will also have subwoofers and an equalizer built in, and a million cassettes on a computer. There are no roads on the moon, either, so a person just goes where he wants, free as a bird. All this adds up to a bright future for me AND ANYONE WHO DISAGREES IS A SUCKER, BUDDY BOY!

ON AVENTURE BOO

Vote Nate for President Dude

■ This reporter met the aforementioned student in Mrs. Arama's third-period cafeteria study hall. Following is the transcript of the taped interview. There were no books in evidence in Mr. Fisher's vicinity.

NATE FISHER: Joel, what's happening. Hi, Mrs. Arama, you look really nice today.

MRS. ARAMA: Thanks, Nate. Get your feet off the table, people eat there.

JOEL: What inner drive compelled you to run for class president?

NATE: Extra credit. Totally blew the American Government test.

JOEL: What do you hope to accomplish as leader of your class?

NATE: Liberation of the masses! A TV in every class! Free doughnuts in homeroom! A car for every student! Parties! If I'm elected there will be serious parties, man.

JOEL: How do you hope to defeat your competition, Amber Hoffman? She runs steering committee, she's ranked number one academically and she's our student-teacher-parent liaison.

NATE: Oh, well, her taste in music is terrible. And even if she has the brainiac vote, I'm pretty sure I can count on the the geeks, the independents and the stoners.

AMY MATTHEWS: Hi, Nate.

NATE: Hi, Amy, I like your hair.

JOEL: How would you sum up your political platform?

NATE: It's like everybody thinks teenagers are selfish and shallow But once we finally get enough TV, doughnuts, cars and parties, maybe we can prove them wrong. Nate Fisher for President! I rock! Woohoo! Hi, Melissa.

Hey Ilya,

Sorry to hear about your grandmother's accident.
I hope she's okay now. I fell down the steps once
and broke my arm, but I saved the cast because
all my friends signed it. I still have it in my
memento box.

That's so cool that both your grandparents live
next door. None of mine are still alive. Most of
them died before I was born or when I was a
baby. I kind of remember my grandmother Fisher.
She was my dad's mother. She was alive till I
was like 5. She used to live with us but she
stayed in her room all the time cause she was sick.
I remember she used to keep her teeth in a glass in
the bathroom and yell at me and Nate all the time
for being loud.

My parents just finished fixing up her old room
for the new baby, who is due any day now. You
wouldn't believe how HUGE my mom is! She can
barely get up off a chair. My dad keeps calling
her his little stuffed sausage. It's pretty funny.

To answer your question from your last letter—
yes, I DO like Michael Jackson. Have you seen
the Billie Jean video? It's really neat! I got the
Thriller album for my birthday this year. I also
like Hall and Oates, The Go-Gos and The Police.
Nate took me to see The Police in concert. They
were AWESOME! Do you like them?

Oh! Before I forget, I was reading some stuff about Russia at the library and wanted to ask you — is it true you guys have "White Nights" where it stays bright all day and all night? I've never heard of that before! That is soooo neat! The latest it's ever stayed light over here is like 9:00 PM during Daylight Savings Time. Do you have Daylight Savings time in Russia?

I also read how your metro stations are really nice with chandeliers and paintings in them. I rode on a subway once in NY when we went to see my dad's cousin and it was totally gross. My mom made us sit on napkins so we wouldn't get dirty and I STILL got gum on my pants!

Anyways, my dad is yelling for me to take out the trash so I should probably close up.

"Talk" to ya later!

David

P.S. Thanks for the rubles. They're so neat!

1983 | RUTH AND NATHANIEL HAVE CLAIRE, AN UNEXPECTED ADDITION TO THE FAMILY.

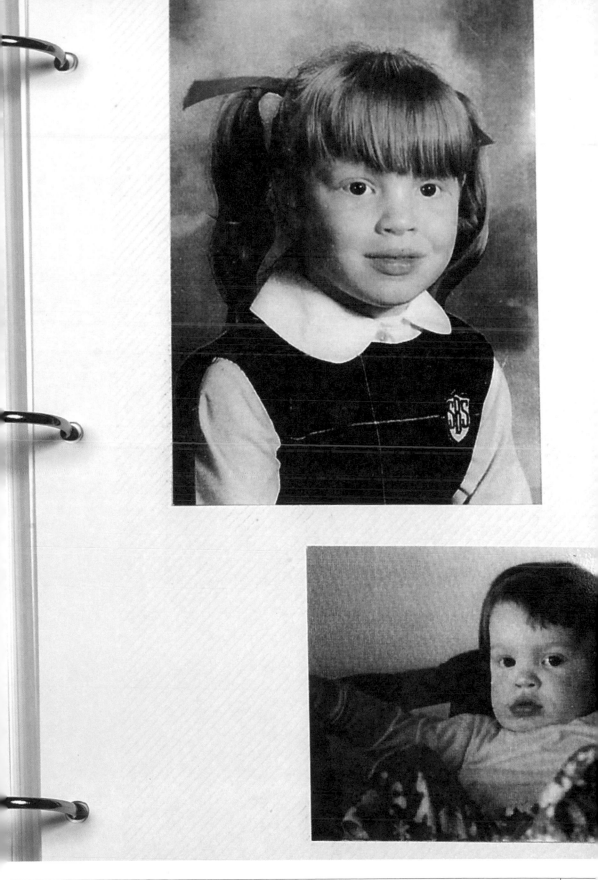

Joyous Tidings of the Season!

What a busy year it's been,
1983!
Lots of changes, lots of growth,
Such activity!

Nate is graduating soon,
From high school, nonetheless!
He'll be going off to college,
Where? is anybody's guess.

David's doing well in school,
But high grades are not all—
He played "Professor Higgins"
In the musical last fall!

Our lives were changed forever
When a princess, sweet and fair,
Came from Heaven this year to live with us—
Our brand-new baby Claire!

Her hair's red like her Mommy's,
Her smile's like her Dad's,
And her brothers love her bundles,
Even when she's bad.

Highlights of the year include
A trip to Yellowstone—
Nate's brand-new motorcycle—
And a puppy followed David home!

We're busy, always busy,
So now we have to run!
But we wish you and those you love
A season full of fun!

Merry Christmas
from
NATHANIEL, RUTH, NATE, DAVID, CLAIRE & OUR PUPPY LANCELOT

THE BHAGAVAD GITA

INVISIBLE BEFORE BIRTH ARE ALL
BEINGS AND AFTER DEATH INVISIBLE
AGAIN. THEY ARE SEEN BETWEEN
TWO UNSEENS. WHY IN THIS TRUTH
FIND SORROW?

Roof of Home Catches Fire in Pacific Palisades

By Adam Roth

The roof of a home in Pacific Palisades burst into flames Thursday night. The cost in damages is estimated to be $150,000.

Heavy smoke was reported to be coming from a house on the 1100 block of Abersham Drive just before 10:40 p.m. Firefighters arrived to find the roof engulfed in flames, officials said.

They extinguished the blaze within 30 minutes and spent the next several hours cleaning up.

The house belongs to Bernard and Margaret Chenowith. "I feel emotionally violated," said Margaret Chenowith, "and I should know about that subject, since in my practice as a psychologist I am constantly treating people who've been emotionally violated."

The cause of the fire is unknown. Arson investigators were called out but were unable to determine the cause of the fire by Friday afternoon. Arson cannot be ruled out at this point, and the investigation will continue, officials said.

1986 | AFTER BILLY ATTEMPTS TO BURN THE FAMILY HOUSE DOWN, BRENDA STAYS HOME TO LOOK AFTER HIM.

Brenda Chenowith
1172 Abersham Drive
Pacific Palisades, CA
90272

Dear Ms. Chenowith,
We were sorry to learn of your recent decision not to attend
Yale University. We had looked forward to your participation in the
Fall 1986 freshman orientation.

We realize that choosing an institution of learning is a difficult task,
and that deciding when to undertake one's undergraduate studies
can be equally difficult.

We do hope you will consider Yale in the future. Unfortunately, it is
not our policy to accept deferments, but we welcome you to reapply.

Best of luck,

Pamela Shreve

Pamela Shreve
Admissions

1980 | THE DEFINITIVE HEARSE SINCE 1938, SAYERS & SCOVILL'S VICTORIA LANDAU REMAINS A PREMIUM CHOICE.

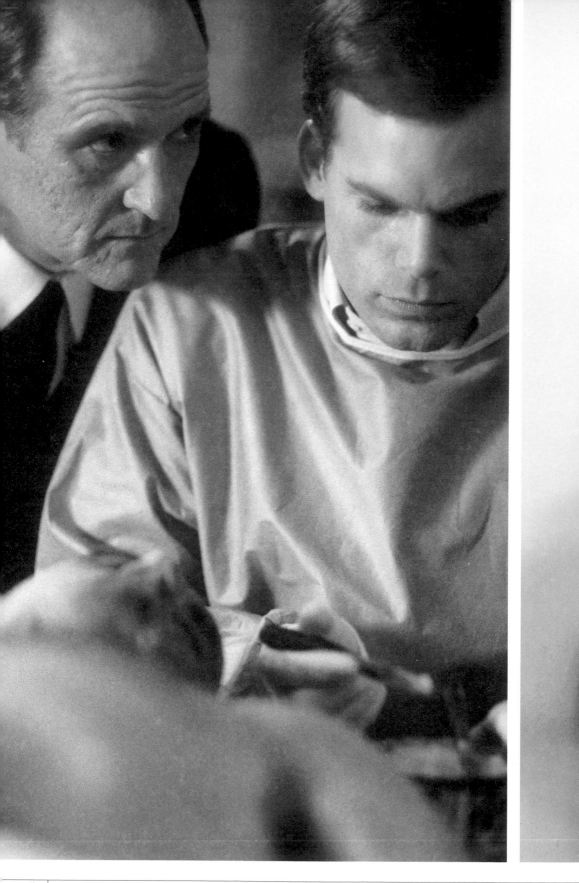

1989 | AT 20, DAVID JOINS THE FAMILY BUSINESS TO WORK WITH HIS FATHER.

Other kids my age were going to frat parties. I was draining corpses and refashioning severed ears out of wax.
~ DAVID

Dearest Keith,

You have to forgive your father for reacting the way he did when you told him about your new lifestyle. Both of us are still trying to understand why you would make a choice like this, but your father is quick to anger. It's just his way. We both know this. Honestly, if you stand by your word and never set foot in our house again, it would break my heart. And your Grandma's heart as well. This is your home, son, and it always will be. Just let things cool down for a while and then come home for Christmas. I will make your favorite sweet potato pie and you and your father can make up. I can tell every time I look at him he's missing hearing from you. You are his only boy, and he loves you more than anything and nothing will ever change that.

Love,
Mom

Dear Mom,

I'm sitting here at a desk in the Irvine library. It's so quiet, you wouldn't believe it. I think I can almost hear some voices down at the circulation desk but that's it. It's like being inside an Egyptian pyramid being in this place.

Don't worry about Dad and me. I will find a way to explain it to him better someday. It's my fault he got mad. I think I was almost yelling at him when I told him I was gay because I was already so scared he was going to hit me or something. I will definitely come home for Christmas, Mom, you don't even have to make anything special for me.

I have actually already written Dad a long letter apologizing for the way I handled the whole situation. I was just waiting to send it. I will send it tomorrow and then everything will be okay.

Mom, you are the best person in the world. Thank you for taking the time to write me a letter. I am so lucky to have you and Dad in my life. I'm trying my best.

Yesterday, I met Andrew Young after he spoke to my class about human rights. He is a great man. He said there are still a lot of challenges facing African Americans. He said the fight for civil rights isn't over, but instead it's just beginning. I told him I think he's right and he shook my hand and told me I was a fine young man.

You can tell Dad that last part if you want.

Love, Keith

Mother's Day Movie Report

The movie that I watched with my mom over Mother's Day weekend is *My Girl*. My mother picked this movie because it's about a girl who lives in a funeral home. I do have some things in common with the lead character Vada but mostly we're different.

One similarity between me and Vada is that she wants to be a writer and I do, too. She takes a creative writing class over the summer with a bunch of weird adults instead of trying to make friends with the mean girls at school. She writes bad poems until something very tragic happens. I won't say what it was. Then she is able to tap into sadness and write a good poem at the end.

Vada keeps visiting the doctor because every time someone dies and comes to the funeral home, Vada thinks that she is dying from the same thing. But it's obvious she just wants attention. Her mother is dead and her father works all the time and she doesn't have any brothers or sisters. My brothers are much older than me and my dad works a lot, too. But I know he's doing it to support the family. My mother says Vada was a hypochondriac but that I hardly ever get sick, thank goodness.

Vada tries to bond with Shelly, a lady who works at the funeral home doing makeup. There's a whole part of the movie where the dad falls in love with Shelly. Then Vada gets very jealous and tries to break them up and goes psycho at the carnival bumper-car ride. None of this has ever happened to me and I think if my mother died and my father started dating again I wouldn't be such a baby about it.

I would say that's the main difference between me and Vada—everyone treats her like she's much younger than she really is (11). Her dad and Shelly don't tell her that they plan to get married, even though Shelly is clearly wearing a diamond engagement ring!

Even though the movie was unrealistic at times, it was still pretty good. It got very sad at the end and my mom started crying all over the place like she always does! But I remembered that it was just a movie like I always do.

Dear Claire,

I guess we both know by now that I didn't invite you to my sleepover. My mom wanted me to apologize for this, so sorry. Even though you give me the creeps, my mom made me realize I should get over it. You probably don't sleep in a waterbed filled with formaldehyde, and you can't help the business your family is in because you were born into it. I also realize that you probably don't know how to kill people by thinking about them, and that you probably didn't lose your virginity to a ghost. I was being stupid when I thought these things, and when I said these things to my friends at school, and when I made the decision not to invite you to my sleepover. Please accept my apology, and I look forward to the friendship we can share until my next sleepover. Please also thank your mother for being in touch with my mother about this whole thing. She's been a great help in getting it cleared up.

Sincerely,

Rebecca

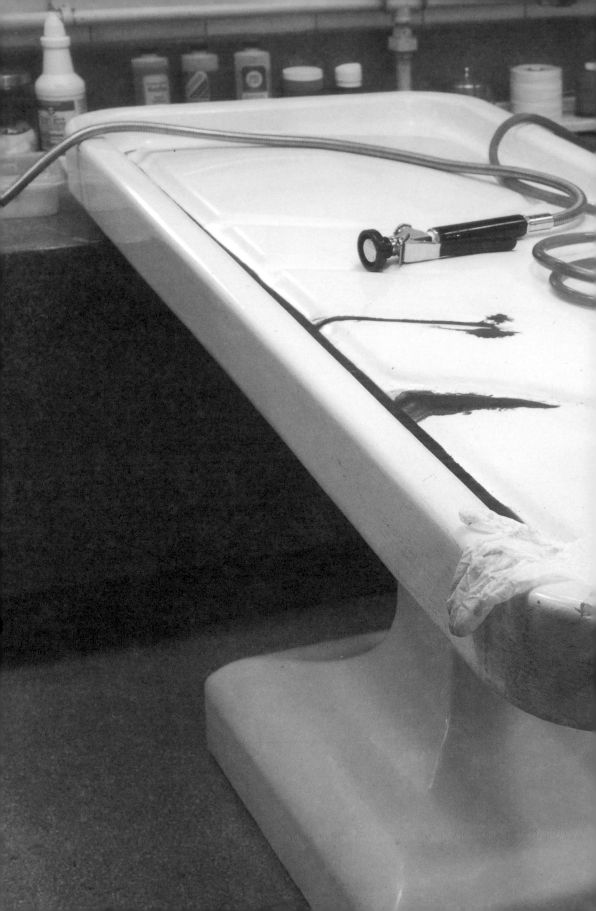

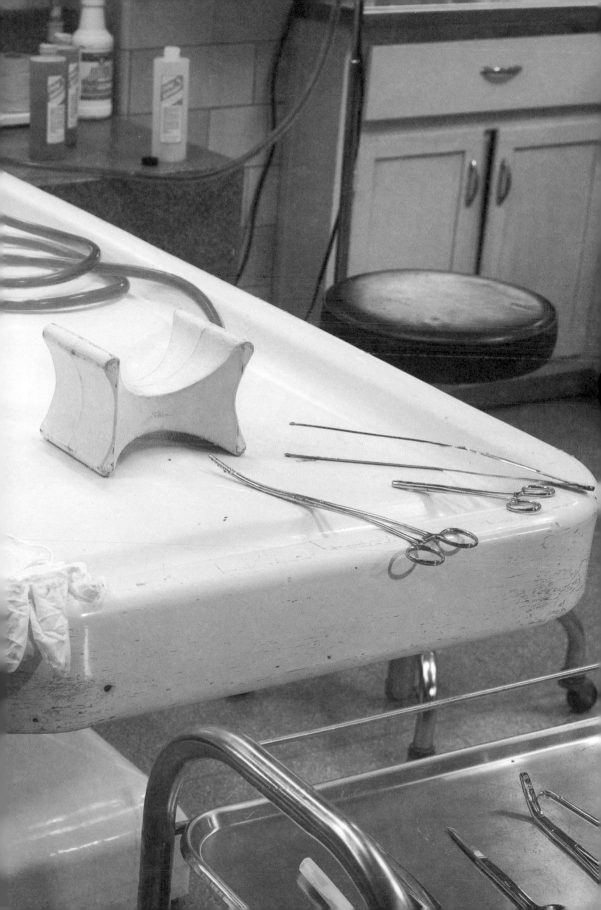

December 17, 1996

Dear Mr. Fisher,

I made it through my first semester at Cypress. I know I told you I was worried about Anatomy, but it wasn't that hard at all. Just a lot of Latin to memorize—you know how it goes. The final exam was this week, and they haven't posted our grades yet but I'm pretty sure I aced it. In high school I never paid attention in biology class, but it gets a whole lot more interesting when you know you'll be going inside. I got to come face to face with my first dead body (aside from my father) in Restorative Arts 1—a young man who died of a drug overdose. I mostly had to clean him up, make him look okay for a viewing. I guess they don't give us the gunshot victims and stuff until next year. The only class I didn't like was Regulatory Environment, where you learn the governmental regulations and all that. But I understand why it's important.

I want to thank you again for paying my tuition here and for suggesting this line of work to me in the first place. Watching how you do your job, I can see how much funeral directors help people, and I would like that kind of work for myself. My mom wants me to pass along her best wishes. I won't let you down. Have a good Christmas with your family.

Sincerely,

Federico

March 3, 1997

Dear Mr. Fisher,

I'm almost done with my final semester at Cypress. It's been so incredible. I never realized I had such a knack for this kind of work. Clinical Embalming and the Restorative Art Lab have been my favorite courses by far. I love the hands-on stuff. And one of my instructors said he's never seen a student with such natural ability. Not bad, huh? In Restorative Art Lab last week, we worked on a homeless woman who had been hit by a train. She was in five pieces and her face was gone and there were no photos to work from. It was a tough one, but I couldn't wait for the instructor to stop talking so I could start working on her.

In the beginning, I was mostly thinking about tests and grades and making you and my mom proud. But I was up late the other night working on a project and I started thinking about the guy on the slab and how I want his family to feel when they see him. I almost got the chills—not in a creepy way, but because everything changed for me right then, and the reality of what I'm going to do for a living set in. If everything goes according to plan, I'll graduate in June and I can start working for you. I'm really looking forward to it. My mother sends her best wishes.

Sincerely,
Rico

The visitors, faculty, and graduating class of

CYPRESS COLLEGE

proudly announce the first convocation

of the

twenty-ninth commencement exercises

Saturday, May twenty-fifth

Nineteen hundred and ninety-seven

at ten o'clock in the morning

FEDERICO DIAZ

KIMMEL'S CORNER

Hello, one and all! Great apologies for skipping the May newsletter, as many of you know the fire over at the Yarn Barn took precedence. How wonderful that everyone was able to pitch in and help Emil and the gang with the clean-up. At times like this it is so comforting to know that we can count on one another.

And now on to "more important" things - announcements!

We have an overstock of MUNG BEANS in the store room so if you have a place to keep them (remember cool and dry!!!!!!) feel free to take your (fair) share!

Sadly, our RECIPE RECEPTACLE is empty! Have you noticed the brown box near the muffin kiosk? Well fill it up! I am sure you might have wonderful organic, vegetarian or "otherwise" recipes that you wish to share with others. Just drop them off at your next visit.

MENSTRUAL SPONGES have arrived! For years the women of ancient Egypt of the Nile valley stanched their moon flows with all natural sea sponges. Now the women of Seattle can do the same. Simply use, rinse, and re-use for a "greener" future.

JOIN A DREAM GROUP - Work with the images, feelings and associations from your dreams and thoughts of others in a supportive group. Gain insight from the open discussion. Check out Jasper's beautiful posters for this newly formed group on your way in.

KALE, KALE THE GANG'S ALL HERE! (the new produce manager, that is!)
His name is Nathaniel "Nate" Fisher and he's a new arrival in the Seattle area, so if you see him arranging clementines, feel free to introduce yourself. Now I'll let him say a "few words".

Keep it Green,
Lisa

✌ ✌

Hello one and all. My name is Nate Fisher and I am thrilled to have been invited to join your community. I have a fair bit of experience in the sales world. Some of you may recognize me from Rounder Records, the largest used record store in the Seattle-metro area. However, the organics world itself is new to me, so I am looking for everyone's advice, input, etc., and would love to meet each and every one of you.

P.S. Looking for small one-bedroom house! (I am currently in a temporary roommate situation but if anyone knows of a small home under $600/month I am VERY interested.)

SHE SAW THINGS DIFFERENTLY
By Claire Fisher, grade 11

When she woke up that day, she could see perfectly out of one eye.

Kali had terrible eyesight, and had been wearing glasses since she was nine years old. Coke-bottle, glass-brick, lenses-as-thick-as-French-toast glasses that were so heavy they had already dented her nose for life. Friends of hers at school (or more appropriately, the other antisocial losers who sat with her in the back of the class) were always urging her to get contact lenses, or even laser surgery. *You'd be so cute!* they said, smiling blankly like those people who say "hello" every time you walk into the Gap. As if being cute was something she even wanted. She just smiled back at them, attempting to match their peculiar brainless vacancy, and lied about having some rare condition that kept her from ever letting anything touch her eyes. The truth was she liked wearing the coke bottle glasses because they kept some people from bothering her. Not all people, but every little bit helps.

So, anyway:

When Kali woke up on this seemingly ordinary day, she could see perfectly out of one eye. Of course, since it was only one eye and the other one was blind-as-a-bat-as-usual, it took her some time to realize what was going on. She dug through the half-empty Diet Cokes and totally empty Tylenol PM bottles on her bedside table for her glasses, and stumbling on her way to the bathroom, shoved them onto her face. She switched on the bathroom light and stared at herself in the mirror, making her ritual Dawn Weiner face—she had never been able to look at herself in a mirror without making a face. It was too naked, too creepy, too embarrassing. But the face that looked back at her from the mirror wasn't right, somehow. Something was off—what was it? There was the standard nursing home hair, the puffy morning face, the weirdly translucent skin that she sometimes loved but more often thought made her look like a vampire, and denting her nose, of course, the dorky Jan Brady frames, chosen on purpose because they were so intentionally anti-fashion. Nothing was different, but something about the whole picture seemed strange. Out of kilter. Maybe even possibly... *interesting.*

Maybe I'm still high from last night, she thought. *Maybe this is a dream.* Then, brightening: *Maybe I've had a stroke and now I won't have to go to gym class any more.*

Later, she sat at the breakfast table, playing her part in her mother's long-running morning show:

I don't see why you can't make more of an effort to look nice. (translation: *You look terrible.*)

I can make more of an effort, I just choose not to. (I don't care.)

But people form their first impressions of you based on your appearance. (But people will think I'm a bad mother.)

I'm not interested in people who are that shallow. (You are a bad mother.)

Staring into her bowl of soggy cornflakes to avoid looking at her mother's face—which always made her want to cry, and it was just too early in the morning to feel so maudlin—Kali thought her glasses must be dirty. She took them off to clean them, as her mother droned on, oblivious: *I think you're just worried that people won't be interested in you*...

With her glasses off, she suddenly realized: *Oh my God, I can see. Well, sort of.*

She closed one eye, and there it was: the familiar blurriness that the eye doctor said came from watching too much television. Then she closed the other eye—

Whoa.

Life snapped into sharp focus, far clearer than it had ever been, even *with* glasses. It was exhilarating, beautiful, stunning. She was literally stunned.

She just sat there, staring at the corn flakes in the bowl in front of her, and somehow she could see every grain, every detail of texture, color, and shadow. It was unbelievably gorgeous, as if it were being photographed and painted at the same time, illuminated by some mysterious light from another dimension. She was transfixed. It was as if she were looking into a microscope and slowly adjusting the magnification, and she started to be able to see almost every individual cell of each corn flake (do corn flakes *have* cells?) and then each molecule, and then the infinitesimal buzz of actual *atoms*. She began to feel the warmth of steam on her face, and then...

She realized the milk in her cereal bowl was boiling.

Kali, a voice said from far away, alarmed. Apparently her mother had realized it too.

Kali looked up at her, startled, still keeping the other eye, the normal, nearly blind eye, clamped tightly shut. Her mother looked back at her, equally startled, her standard mask of sadness and resignation replaced by a face that seemed suddenly younger, more open, and more curious. Kali gasped. She had never realized how beautiful her mother was, had never noticed the flecks of gold in her mother's green eyes, the lids of which slowly started to flutter like a bee's wings. She had never observed the way the morning light danced like fire through her mother's auburn hair, which, as Kali's vision started to magnify, she could actually see *growing*, pushing itself out of her mother's scalp...

Oh dear, her mother said, putting the back of her hand to her forehead, a suddenly pained expression on her face. Instinctively, Kali looked away.

I've just developed the worst headache. Oh my. I'm going to have to go lie down. And her mother padded out of the kitchen and up the back stairs.

And suddenly Kali knew. She knew she had caused her mother's headache. She knew she could have caused much worse than that, had she wanted to, had she really put her mind to it. And she knew that she had always known, on some deep instinctive level, that she had just been waiting for the day when it would all become clear, frighteningly clear, clearer than she had ever dreamed possible, so clear that the word 'clarity' seemed feeble and useless.

Finally, her life was starting.

Sitting alone in the back of the school bus, hiding behind her glasses, she thought about things she hadn't thought about for a long time. Like playing alone in the back yard when she was little, building an elaborate neighborhood in her sandbox with shoeboxes and her brother's Matchbox cars. A miniature suburb, complete with flowers swiped from her mother's azalea bushes out front. Then building a reservoir behind it all, the dam purposely flawed, so that when she filled it up with the garden hose, she could watch the dam give way and the ensuing deluge destroy the toy homes below, filling her young, not-yet-self-conscious heart with glee. She had been how old, five? Six at the most.

And remembering now, how after the flood washed everything away, and her euphoria was starting to fade, how she had gotten the distinct feeling that someone was watching her. Remembering turning and looking up at the sky, only to see the sky itself split open and reveal a gigantic, placid, single eye, looking back down at her. Curious, amused, without judgment.

Okay, get real. That couldn't have really happened. That was a goofy childhood dream, long forgotten. Or maybe she was hallucinating. Maybe she was just going crazy. Or *maybe...*

Hey, uber-skank. Pull any trains lately? The familiar raspy voice: another daily ritual. Jesus, why were people so predictable?

Kali sighed and looked up into the lopsided grin of Carl Eubanks, white trash stud extraordinaire, leaning over the seat in front of her. She had known Carl since first grade, and he had always been the alpha dog, making himself the center of attention on playgrounds and in hallways, smoking cigarettes since birth, tormenting and terrorizing the weak and sensitive, the overweight, the future homosexuals, the girls who took longer than everyone else to develop. Possessing the foolish arrogance of the naturally strong, the aggressive stupidity of those who everyone else defers to just because they're a little bigger, a little better looking, a little scarier.

Hi, Carl. Is it my imagination, or are you even more of an idiot than you were yesterday?

Carl snorted and revealed more teeth. Whether it was a smile or a bestial display of hostility wasn't entirely clear.

Yeah, right. Bite my crank, uber-skank.

Careful, your Nazi roots are showing.

Carl laughed like he got it, but she knew he didn't. The bus stopped and she looked out the window at the depressing barracks-like structure of Bonaventure High. As Carl stood up, a streak of viciousness flickered across his blandly handsome face.

I wouldn't bang you if you were the last girl on earth.

Kali almost laughed. Was that supposed to hurt her? She smiled at Carl, almost feeling sorry for him and his puffed-up tough guy routine.

Well, I'm sure that'll be a great solace to you behind the counter at McDonald's. Or prison.

She didn't expect what happened next: Carl spat in her face. Before she could even fully process the fact that yes, he had actually spit in her face, he was laughing and getting off the bus. She just sat there, literally stunned for the second time that day, watching him as he ambled toward the school with his ridiculous self-confidence, his offensive assumption that he was better than everyone else *just because he was hot?!*

She realized she simply couldn't let that continue. So she took off her glasses, closed the one eye and focused the other on Carl's blond head as he walked away from her. She knew exactly how to do it. It wasn't concentration exactly; it was more of a surrender, a giving up to the power that was flowing through her, a power that was bigger then she was. It only took a few seconds before Carl stumbled, as if suddenly drunk. His hands reached up and covered his ears, trying to block out the noise. *Poor thing,* she thought. *He doesn't realize it's coming from inside him.* She watched, mesmerized, as his hair burst into flames and he dropped to his knees, screaming. Other students stopped and stared, and then:

Pop. Carl's head exploded in a bright flash and his body drooped to the ground, twitched for a few seconds, then was still. The other students just stood there, dumbstruck, then one usually perky girl in her cheerleading uniform started to scream, realizing that her chest was now spattered with bits of Carl's brain and hair.

Kali took a deep breath. Feeling remarkably refreshed, she put her glasses on, stood up, and got off the bus. For the first time since she could remember, she was actually looking forward to what the day might hold in store for her.

DEAR MS. FISHER:

WHILE YOUR STORY IS QUITE WELL-WRITTEN, I'M AFRAID I CANNOT ALLOW IT TO BE PUBLISHED, FOR THE REASONS I HAVE LISTED BELOW:

1. INAPPROPRIATE LANGUAGE.
2. ALLUSIONS TO DRUG USE.
3. ALLUSIONS TO PROMISCUOUS SEXUAL BEHAVIOR.
4. PREMEDITATED VIOLENCE, BLOOD AND GORE.
5. AN OVERALL DARK AND NIHILISTIC TONE.

I DO FEEL YOU HAVE TALENT, AND I LOOK FORWARD TO OTHER LESS DISTURBING PIECES YOU MIGHT CHOOSE TO SUBMIT TO BONAVENTURE HIGH'S LITERARY MAGAZINE IN THE FUTURE.

SINCERELY,

HELEN BEEKMAN SCHWARTZ
THE CONDOR QUILL

HEY NATE,

I WANT YOU TO KNOW THAT AS I'M WRITING THIS, THERE IS A BIG STEAMING HAMBURGER SITTING ON MY DESK. AND NEXT TO THE BIG HAMBURGER IS A GIGANTIC GLASS OF MILK. I AM GOING TO TAKE A BIG BITE OUT OF THE HAMBURGER NOW. MMMM, THAT WAS GOOD. AND NOW I'M GOING TO WASH IT DOWN WITH SOME MILK. EVEN BETTER. WHICH BRINGS ME TO MY NEXT SUBJECT, WHICH IS NOT SO GOOD, AND WHICH LEAVES A BAD TASTE IN MY MOUTH : YOU. NATE FUCKING FISHER. NATE "I CAN'T COMMIT TO ANYTHING BECAUSE MY CHILDHOOD LEFT ME DAMAGED" FISHER. NATE "I DON'T THINK I CAN HANDLE BEING A FATHER SO I DON'T THINK WE SHOULD HAVE THE BABY, BUT OF COURSE IT'S YOUR DECISION, I'M JUST SAYING IS ALL" FISHER. NATE "OH NOW THAT YOU DIDN'T HAVE THE BABY, I THINK I MIGHT JUST NEED SOME TIME TO MYSELF" FISHER.

DO YOU THINK THAT I MISS YOU? I DO NOT. DO YOU THINK THAT I FEEL HURT AND DESERTED AND ISOLATED? I DO NOT. DO YOU THINK THAT I HAVE EVEN A SHRED OF RESPECT FOR THE WAY YOU TREAT OTHER HUMAN BEINGS? NO, I DO NOT!

TAKE A LOOK AROUND, DAMAGED MAN-CHILD. YOU HAVE MAJOR RELATIONSHIP ISSUES. GODDAMN THIS HAMBURGER IS GOOD.

HOLD ON A SEC WHILE I TAKE ANOTHER BITE. JESUS, I WISH YOU COULD KNOW HOW DELICIOUS THIS MEAT TASTES WHILE I CRAM IT DOWN MY MOUTH AS I WRITE THIS. IF YOU WERE HERE WITH ME, I WOULD CRAM IT DOWN YOUR MOUTH UNTIL YOU CHOKED. OOPS, SORRY, LOOKS LIKE SOME JUICE FROM THE MEAT DRIBBLED ONTO THE PAPER. LET ME JUST WIPE THAT AWAY. OH BOY, THIS IS HOW I LIKE IT, THOUGH, EXTRA RARE. YOU DIDN'T KNOW THAT, DID YOU? YOU DIDN'T KNOW I LIKED MY MEAT LIKE THAT, AND THERE'S A LOT OF OTHER REALLY FUCKING IMPORTANT THINGS YOU DIDN'T KNOW! BECAUSE YOU WERE TOO GODDAMN BUSY LOOKING AT YOUR NAVEL, YOU SANCTIMONIOUS PRICK! CONGRATULATING YOURSELF ON WHAT A SENSITIVE SHIT YOU ARE—NOT LIKE THOSE OTHER MEN.

BUT HERE IS A NEWSFLASH: YOU ARE JUST LIKE THOSE OTHER MEN, ONLY WORSE! BECAUSE YOU'RE A WOLF IN SHEEP'S CLOTHING, PRETENDING TO BE ONE THING AND ACTING LIKE ANOTHER. HERE IS THE TRUTH: YOU ARE A BLAST OF ACID RAIN THAT CAME INTO MY LIFE AND LEFT ME HATING MYSELF FOR EVER HAVING CARED ABOUT YOU. BUT I AM SO OVER THAT NOW. THE ROAD TO RECOVERY HAS BEGUN, AND YOU ARE ALL BUT A BAD FLASHBACK. ISN'T THAT IRONIC? ISN'T THAT JUST THE CRAZIEST DAMN THING, HOW IT ALL TURNED OUT IN THE END? CONSIDERING YOUR FAMILY'S ILLUSTRIOUS BUSINESS. WHAT I AM TRYING TO SAY IS THIS: YOU ARE DEAD TO ME, NATE FISHER. YOU ARE A GODDAMN DEAD MAN WALKING, IS WHAT YOU ARE. SO SEE YOU IN THE AFTERLIFE, PAL.
                                    — NORA

Lis—

Went to hike Granite Mountain with Jim. Be back Monday or Tuesday. That huge Downy Farms shipment doesn't come until Wednesday — the rest of the dept. can take care of itself. Last night was fun. No regrets, but I don't know if it was the smartest thing in the world either, considering everything that's been going on with Denise. But it was good. Have a good weekend.

See you when I get back.

— Nate

Note from therapy session with Jess:
    Get in touch with your true feelings about Nate by writing a letter to him, expressing all the things you never felt you could say.

Mail the letter to yourself.

2000 | WHILE LIVING IN SEATTLE, NATE SLEEPS WITH HIS ROOMMATE, LISA KIMMEL.

Dear Nate,

There are so many things I want to tell you, but I'm just too afraid to say them out loud. I don't know if you're ready to hear them yet, anyway. God, I love you so much. I know on some level you must know that, just as I know that you love me . . . even if you don't know it yet.

My friends keep telling me I'm stupid for loving you so much. That you're an ass and you treat me like shit and you only come to me when you're horny or fucked up. But they don't know you like I do. I know there's a reason you always seek me out. I can feel it when we're together and I know you've felt it too. We're fated for each other, like Radha and Krishna. And like Radha, I can accept your having sex with all the other gopis, knowing that you'll eventually return to me for truly divine love.

Remember that time you broke up with Tessa a few days before my birthday two years ago? Do you think that was a coincidence? I had just been telling you how I was getting a little serious with Foster, and that we were planning on going to Burning Man together. It was the first time since we'd been together that I opened myself up to the possibility of someone else . . . and then suddenly you became available again.

When you came into my room that night before I was supposed to leave and we made love—it was so perfect and so right. I felt so close to you then. I knew I couldn't go with Foster, that I'd be rejecting my soul's code if I did. And even though you got back together with Tessa a few days later, I realized that something in you wanted to keep me available so that when you were ready to let love in, I'd be there. That's why I never cared that you only came to me when you were drunk or pissed or felt rejected, because I knew that the reason you were doing that is because you felt safe with me. And I feel safe with you, Nate. That's why I'm still waiting with open arms. But I want you to know that my arms are starting to get tired. And a part of me wonders if I can hold out for you.

I will admit, I felt a little sad and angry when you just picked up and left a few months ago. I knew you needed time to deal with your father's death and help your family . . . but you could've called, Nate. You could have at least TOLD me that you were moving back—instead of my having to read about it in the co-op newsletter. That really hurt. I deserve better, I know that, but I can't stop loving you. It's so unfair. I want you to feel as bad as I feel. I want you to know what it's like to miss a person so much it hurts. It physically hurts me, Nate. My arms ache, my neck aches, my whole body aches for you. And I just wish that I could HURT you as much as you're hurting me. Sometimes I dream that I'm KILLING you and I watch you squirm and scream as I stick the knife into your heart and I feel so EXHILARATED—like I just stepped out of a natural hot spring that cleansed me of your toxins. And for one blissful moment, I'm free of you! Then I wake up and reality hits and I'm even more miserable than before.

Why won't you love me? WHY?! What is SO wrong with me that you can't see me like I see you? Am I not stupid enough for you? Is that it? Because that seems to be what you're attracted to: stupid, pretty blondes with bouncy breasts. Do you really think they can give you what you need? Are you really THAT fucking shallow?

No one will EVER love you like I do or want to take care of you or clean up your FUCKING puke or fix your FUCKING favorite meals whenever you want. You know, it's funny, my therapist keeps asking me what I get out of being in a relationship with you, and honestly, I don't know anymore. Here I am, this pathetic LOSER, missing you and crying over you and smelling your stupid shirts, while you're off with your new career and your NEW fucking girlfriend. What do you expect me to do? Am I just supposed to say "Great! That's great, Nate. I'll be here when you come to your senses"? Old reliable Lisa, she'll be there when I need her, right? Well, NEWSFLASH ASSHOLE: I'm a person, too! And I FUCKING deserve more. And one day, you're going to realize that, but it'll be too late. It'll be too fucking late.

So fuck you,

Lisa

CONTRACT BETWEEN CLAIRE AND NATHANIEL
ON PURCHASE OF HEARSE

I, Nathaniel Fisher, do hereby cede ownership of one 1972 Superior Cadillac Crown Sovereign Hearse to Claire Fisher on condition that she be responsible for properly maintaining said vehicle (including oil changes every three thousand miles), never drive it in excess of the posted speed limit, never allow hitchhikers or alcoholic beverages to pass through its doors, keep her grade-point average at or above a B, help her mother around the house without complaint, and give her father one hug and one smile per day.

I, Claire Fisher, accept ownership of the hearse according to the above-stated conditions, with the provision that helping my mother around the house does not include doing David's stinky laundry, and that, on occasion, the smile offered to my father may not be of a sincere nature. Also, as owner of the vehicle, I shall be allowed to paint and redecorate it in any fashion I so choose, and my father shall not say a single negative word about it.

I, Nathaniel Fisher, agree to Claire Fisher's provisions, with the condition that, if the hearse is painted anything other than black, it never be parked in front of the Fisher & Sons Funeral Home, but always in the back driveway. Also, if Claire Fisher's smile is not heartfelt, it must be accompanied by a freshly baked chocolate chip cookie.

I, Claire Fisher, agree to park in the driveway behind the house as long as Mom agrees not to hog the whole driveway. Also, the smiles must be accepted as offered, without a cookie, because Claire Fisher does not bake, nor will she ever bake.

Agreed and dated, June 11, 2000
Signed,

Claire Fisher ___Claire Fisher___

Nathaniel Fisher ___Nathanl Fishe___

THOMAS LYNCH BODIES IN MOTION AND AT REST

A FUNERAL IS NOT A GREAT INVESTMENT;
IT IS A SAD MOMENT IN A FAMILY'S
HISTORY. IT IS NOT A HEDGE AGAINST
INFLATION; IT IS A RITE OF PASSAGE. IT
IS NOT A BARGAIN; IT IS AN EFFORT TO
MAKE SENSE OF OUR MORTALITY. IT HAS
LESS TO DO WITH ACTUARIAL PROFITS
AND MORE TO DO WITH ACTUAL LOSSES.
IT IS NOT AN EXERCISE IN SALESMAN-
SHIP; IT IS AN EXERCISE IN HUMANITY.

2000 | ON CHRISTMAS EVE, WHILE DRIVING HIS NEW HEARSE, NATHANIEL FISHER IS HIT BY A BUS AND KILLED.

I bequeath the company Fisher & Sons Funeral Home
and all real property and business interests attached
as follows: Fifty percent to my son David James Fisher
and fifty percent to my son Nathaniel Samuel Fisher

FISHER & SONS

FUNERAL HOME

Our Home Is Still Your Home

...

Fisher & Sons is pleased to announce that, in the wake of the unfortunate passing of Nathaniel Fisher, beloved husband and father, the proud tradition of quality service that you have become accustomed to at Fisher & Sons Funeral Home will continue. I would like to take a moment to introduce myself, David Fisher, the new operator at Fisher & Sons. I will be assisted by my brother and co-operator, Nate Fisher. Since 1941, my family has proudly served the L.A. community with compassionate death care characterized by a highly personal touch.

This is the bus. ~ BRENDA
What bus? ~ NATE
The bus. ~ BRENDA

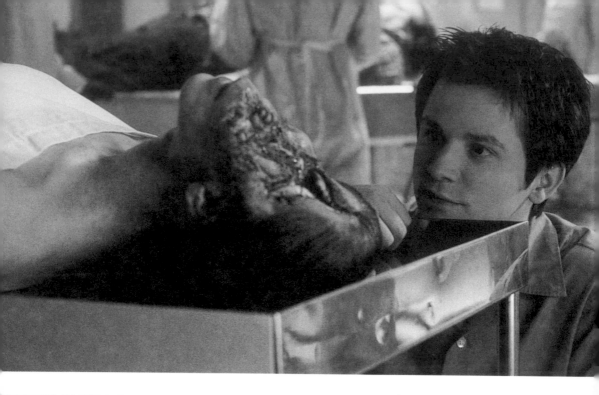

2001 | FEDERICO'S SKILL AT RECONSTRUCTION MAKES HIM ATTRACTIVE TO THE COMPETITORS OF FISHER & SONS.

I'd start with some heavy duty armature material and plaster of Paris. Mastic compound for her face . . . Tissue builder and wax for her features. I'd finish her off with a good sealer. . . . A little airbrushing and a high-quality foundation and she's good to go. ~ FEDERICO

FISHER & SONS FUNERAL HOME

RECEIPT OF CREMATED REMAINS AND RELEASE OF LIABILITY

The undersigned hereby certify that they have the legal right to take custody and make disposition of the cremated remains of the deceased and hereby acknowledge receipt of the cremated remains of

NAME OF DECEDENT:

The undersigned further assumes full responsibility for the lawful and proper disposition of said cremated remains.

The undersigned hereby agree to indemnify and hold harmless the above named cemetery/funeral home, its agents and employees from any and all liability, including reasonable attorney fees, and against any loss it or any of them may sustain in connection with the receipt of, shipment of, or disposition of said cremated remains.

Further, the above named cemetery/funeral home shall be held harmless from any defects or faults of any container not supplied by the cemetery/funeral home.

DATED THIS   DAY OF

ADDRESS:

| Street | City | State | Zip |

SIGNATURE:

| Authorized Representative | Photo ID Number |

WITNESS:

| Representative of Cemetery / Funeral Home |

DO NOT DESTROY

THIS ENVELOPE contains the REMOVAL PERMIT from the Department of Health, State of California, for the Cremated Remains of

Donna Sakima

Cremation Number: 08654

FROM
We Care Cremations, Inc.
5337 Rosemary Lane - Los Angeles, CA 90211

DO NOT DESTROY

THIS ENVELOPE contains the REMOVAL PERMIT from the Department of Health, State of California, for the Cremated Remains of

Laura Kotcharian

Cremation Number: 47382   Date: 04/02/2001

From
We Care Cremations , Inc.
5337 Rosemary Lane – Los Angeles, CA 90211

DO NOT DESTROY

THIS ENVELOPE contains the REMOVAL PERMIT from the Department of Health, State of California, for the Cremated Remains of

Hugh Salamon

Cremation Number: 29031

FROM
We Care Cremations, Inc.
5337 Rosemary Lane - Los Angeles, CA 90211

DO NOT DESTROY

THIS ENVELOPE contains the REMOVAL PERMIT from the Department of Health, State of California, for the Cremated Remains of

Jerald Goodman

Cremation Number: 11029

FROM
We Care Cremations , Inc.
5337 Rosemary Lane - Los Angeles, CA 90211

DO NOT DESTROY

THIS ENVELOPE contains the REMOVAL PERMIT from the Department of Health, State of California, for the Cremated Remains of

Vito Mirabella

Cremation Number: 383675   Date: 02/05/2001

From
We Care Cremations , Inc.
5337 Rosemary Lane – Los Angeles, CA 90211

DO NOT DESTROY

THIS ENVELOPE contains the REMOVAL PERMIT from the Department of Health, State of California, for the Cremated Remains of

Randy Sayer

Cremation Number: 10030

FROM
We Care Cremations, Inc.
5337 Rosemary Lane - Los Angeles, CA 90211

DO NOT DESTROY

THIS ENVELOPE contains the REMOVAL PERMIT from the Department of Health, State of California, for the Cremated Remains of

Alan Connell

Cremation Number: 5847438   Date: 09/12/2000

From
We Care Cremations , Inc.
5337 Rosemary Lane – Los Angeles, CA 90211

DO NOT DESTROY

THIS ENVELOPE contains the REMOVAL PERMIT from the Department of Health, State of California, for the Cremated Remains of

Geoffrey Haley

Cremation Number: 78922

FROM
We Care Cremations , Inc.
5337 Rosemary Lane - Los Angeles, CA 90211

DO NOT DESTROY

THIS ENVELOPE contains the REMOVAL PERMIT from the Department of Health, State of California, for the Cremated Remains of

Manuel Baca

Cremation Number: 372843   Date: 01/01/2001

From
We Care Cremations , Inc.
5337 Rosemary Lane – Los Angeles, CA 90211

For twenty years I lived my life like a man.
When are you gonna start? ~ PACO

A Call to Arms:
Protect the Independent Funeral Home!

An essay by David Fisher of Fisher & Sons Funeral Home

Editor's note: After Mr. Fisher's fiery speech at the Southwest Funeral Directors Association Convention in Las Vegas, we asked him to put his background and his views in print, so we can get to know this inspiring speaker better.

My grandfather established Fisher & Sons in 1941 and passed it on to my father in 1967. Back then, a typical day for my dad would be: breakfast with the Rotary Club, meet with a family at 10, lunch with his own family or at a coffee shop with buddies—maybe some of you who are reading this. At 1 P.M., there would probably be a funeral, at 4 P.M. he might embalm, and so on. He knew his competition; he was probably friends with them. They were independent funeral home owners, too.

When I went to mortuary school to follow in his footsteps, my classmates and I were proud to be in a profession with integrity. We had dreams of expanding and improving our services. We planned to introduce more gracious viewing rooms, perhaps even aquariums in the waiting areas. Little did we know that within a decade, our dreams would be viciously attacked by bloodthirsty corporate pirates.

They took us by surprise and we haven't defended ourselves very well. We have to ask ourselves, Why have we been doormats? Whether it's because of good manners or fear or apathy, it's time to wake up and smell the coffee.

As family-run funeral homes, we stand alone against multinational conglomerates, such as Kroehner, who have identified death as the possible source of incredible profit. They will go to ANY lengths to create a monopoly in the death care industry (DCI). The key word here is "industry." If it brings to your mind pictures of factories and assembly lines, you're on the right track.

Because these people didn't learn about death care the way we did, in mortuary school, sharing high hopes and excitement with other students. They were not guided by experienced fathers or uncles or mentors. They never stood by shattered parents and watched a tiny white casket lowered into the earth. No, what companies like Kroehner did was go to McDonald's. This is unbelievable but true. They believe that they can sell funerals like fast food giants sell hamburgers, large fries and milkshakes to fatten the bank accounts of their executives and shareholders. Profit is all they care about.

Crazy, you may say. We have carefully cultivated relationships with the public and other independent merchants connected with the DCI. Kroehner et al. could never compete with our sincerity and individual attention. And even if some of us do sell out, surely there's enough business to go around.

But there isn't. The truth is, there are only about 6,800 deaths a day in America. It's a stable market—you can always count on death and taxes—but it's not flexible. That is, if we don't manage to land a client, that chance is gone. That sale is, so to speak, dead. We are NOT restaurants, where customers may return to try another meal in a week or so. This is why our current situation is so dangerous. Kroehner doesn't live and let live.

Instead, they aim not so much to shut us down (although they will if they have to—just ask a hundred now-defunct funeral homes across the country) as to acquire us. To manage us. To make us part of their system and deceive the public into thinking we are still independent neighborhood folks who will care for their deceased in the same cherished small-town American tradition.

In reality, once part of the monopoly, we would secretly transport the loved one—at great expense to the client—to a central warehouse to be treated like an anonymous ham-burger among many other anonymous hamburgers in the hands of anonymous technicians who neither know nor care who this hamburger was.

Let me tell you the story of one body returned from such a facility to an acquired funeral home for burial. The funeral director opened the casket to find the poor old man completely naked with his hair uncombed! This is an example of one large corporation's respect for the dead. While I'm not suggesting we include these anecdotes in conversation with the recently bereaved, it couldn't hurt to mention a few of the less shocking details for the client's own protection.

If all we had to fight were incompetence and lack of conscience, we could survive. But this situation is more com-plex, because in a takeover, not only the funeral home is acquired, but its suppliers as well. Chemicals, caskets, liners, florists, limousines, dispatchers, drivers, hearses, etc. may all belong to the monopoly. Hold out and you may find your reasonable prices undercut by 50 percent. You may find cavity fluid costs jacked up 200 percent. You may suddenly find a health inspector at your door. Plus, Kroehner and its cronies have lobbyists in Washington to ensure their profit margins, which last year were between 25 and 41 percent.

Our predicament is not hopeless. This is exactly NOT the time to throw in your latex gloves. "Consolidate or die," the chains tell us. Is this true? No. Although they often hold key properties in key markets, they still do not control even 40 percent of the funerals in this country. If they keep undercutting our prices, they will keep undercutting their profits.

In conclusion, these predator companies are driven by greed and answer to stockholders. What we have to offer as independent funeral homes may have no dollar value but counts for everything to someone whose life has been altered forever by the death of a brother, a sister, a parent, a friend. These are the people we answer to, and it is a strength no Kroehner can match.

Bereavement can force y

directly, compelling you

where there may not ha

u to look at your life
to find a purpose in it
e been one before.

www.theplanprogram.org

2001 | RUTH TAKES A JOB AT A FLOWER SHOP AND ATTENDS A SELF-EMPOWERMENT SEMINAR CALLED *THE PLAN.*

THE PLAN

You want me to complain. All right then, fuck this. Fuck you. Fuck all of you with your sniveling self-pity. And fuck all your lousy parents. Fuck my lousy parents while we're at it. Fuck my selfish Bohemian sister and her fucking bliss. Fuck my legless grandmother. Fuck my dead husband. And my lousy children with their nasty little secrets. ~ RUTH

SHIFTS ARE THE DIRECT CAUSE FOR
NEW AND UNIQUE KIND OF FREEDO
AND POWER. THE FREEDOM TO BE
ABSOLUTELY AT EASE NO MATTER
WHERE YOU ARE, WHO YOU'RE WIT
OR WHAT THE CIRCUMSTANCE --
THE POWER TO BE IN ACTION EFFE
TIVELY IN THOSE AREAS OF YOUR
LIFE THAT ARE IMPORTANT TO YOU

TAKE THE NEXT STEP TO A BRIGHT
FUTURE.

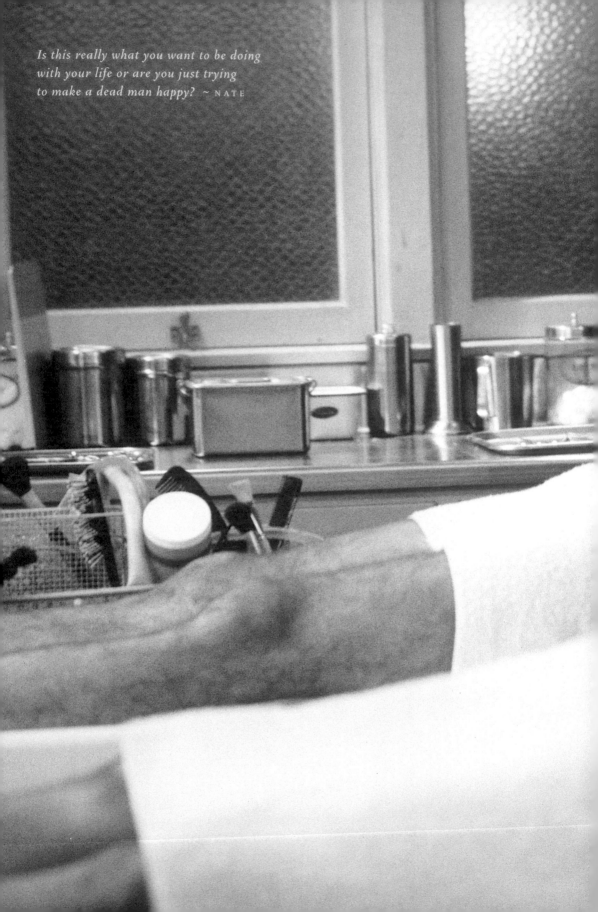

Is this really what you want to be doing
with your life or are you just trying
to make a dead man happy? ~ NATE

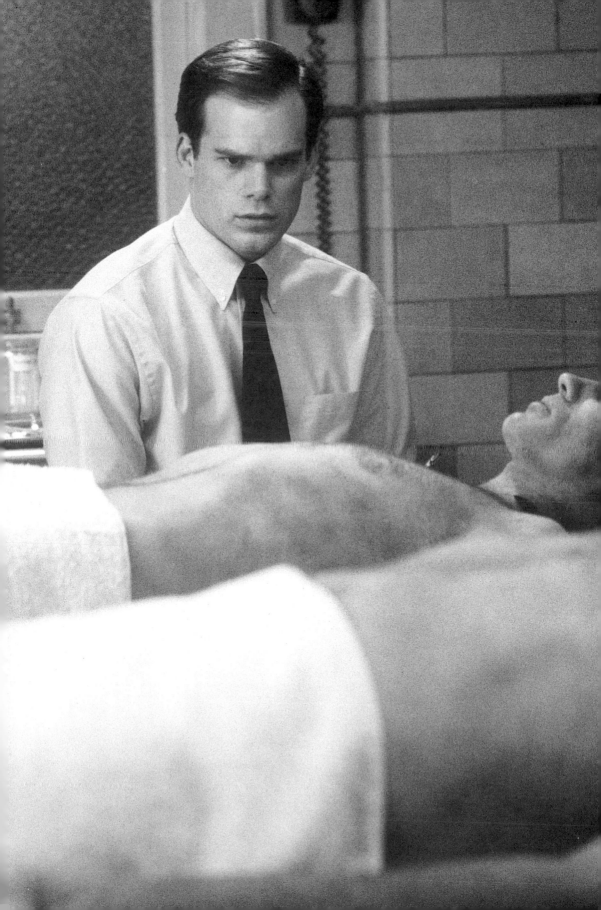

C. S. LEWIS **A GRIEF OBSERVED**

IT IS OFTEN THOUGHT THAT THE DEAD
SEE US. AND WE ASSUME, WHETHER
REASONABLY OR NOT, THAT IF THEY SEE
US AT ALL THEY SEE US MORE CLEARLY
THAN BEFORE.

You wake up one day and your baby's stolen a foot.
Where have I been? ~ RUTH

DATE: February 5, 2001
STUDENT: Claire Fisher

NOTES:

My first session with Ms. Fisher was a little rocky. Initially I found it very difficult to negotiate around her sarcasm and obvious resentment about being "forced" (her word) into meeting with me. When I mentioned that several people were concerned for her well being, she likened their interest to Hitler's interest in the Jews. Later, when I questioned her about the details concerning the foot incident—as to why she stole the foot and what statement she was trying to make by putting it in a classmate's locker, she claimed she was "protesting Footlocker's inability to sell a decent-priced sneaker."

Once I dug a little deeper, however, some deep-seeded issues began to reveal them-selves. I asked her about college and her plans for the future—and that was clearly a "hot button" subject. Ms. Fisher suddenly got very animated and upset. She wanted to know why everyone was suddenly so interested in her and what she does with the rest of her life when she was "basically invisible" for the last seventeen years. When I pressed her further on the matter, she got visibly emotional. She said she felt her father was trying to manipulate her from the grave. (Mr. Fisher was killed in a car accident this past Christmas Eve.) She expressed resentment that her brothers were bequeathed the family business, whereas she was only offered a college educa-tion. She was especially resentful of her older brother Nate.

Unfortunately, I didn't have time to delve further into the matter, as I was running late for another appointment. However, it is clear to me that the death of Ms. Fisher's father has affected her deeply and, most likely, her recent lashing out stems from that.

In closing, though I do not feel Ms. Fisher poses any serious threat to herself or others, she does exhibit signs of distress and mild clinical depression, and I feel she would benefit greatly from regular sessions. I, therefore, recommend that she continue on with me for the remainder of the school year.

SIGNATURE: _GARY DEITMAN_

Gary Deitman

w YOU WITH
elly SHIRT Girl @lunch.
u MAKE A CUTE
♡ couple ♡
veryone in this trig class
s fast asleep but Me.
he only thing that is
eeping me AWAKE (!)
s the fact that Mrs.
ierney keeps
slurring
ter words.

And 4 some reason her hair looks like this today ◠◡

EVERY ONE KNOWS MRS. T IS A RAGING DRUG ADDICT. DON'T WORRY ABOUT MAKING ME WAIT AFTER SCHOOL. WE'LL GET TO THE BOARDWALK AT THE SAME TIME THE SUN SETS. THAT'S WHEN ALL THE BEST FREAKS COME OUT ANYWAY. THEN ANDY KNOWS ABOUT AN AFTERHOURS WAREHOUSE PARTY IN VENICE. BY THE WAY, BELLY SHIRT GIRL SAYS HI.

I can't ditch last period & go to the beach.
I have to finish that ceramics project.
If I do don't turn it in today. I'll get
an incomplete in art. and people who
can't get an A in **ART** shouldn't be
allowed to leave the house without
Adult supervision ...

I hate using the pottery wheel.
The foot pedal keeps getting jammed
and my bowls look completely spastic.

plus, I feel
like Demi Moore
in Ghost.

OH MY GOD!
I hope she's @ the
party tonight !!!!
she has the tightest
Abs, so she must be
excellent company.
Apparently the
Varsity track team
thinks so ....

If we go to that party
it gives us like 6 hrs. to
KILL. I might need
to make a brief
appearance @ home.

THERE IS NO FUCKING WAY I'M LETTING YOU
GO HOME ON A FRIDAY NIGHT. I'LL KEEP
YOU ENTERTAINED FOR 6 HOURS. WE'LL GET
SOME FOOD, MAYBE SEE A MOVIE OR TAKE
THE OPPORTUNITY TO VISIT ONE OF OUR LOCAL
STATE PARKS AFTER THE RANGERS HAVE
GONE HOME. BRAD PITT HAS TIGHT ABS TOO
AND YOU DON'T SEEM TO MIND. CALL ME
WHEN YOU'RE READY TO GO. I LOVE YOU.

```
billybatty:    claire help help me claire oh god help
icdeddpeople:  what r u ok?
billybatty:    no i am so totally fucking bored i'm watching game shows
icdeddpeople:  billy u scared the shit out of me
billybatty:    there's a schizo here who know the answers before the questions.
               THAT is scary
icdeddpeople:  oh man true
billybatty:    how r u
icdeddpeople:  totally fucking bored
billybatty:    shooting any pix?
icdeddpeople:  yeah but they suck. except this one of a bad transvestite i saw
               at the mall.
billybatty:    bad like evil?
icdeddpeople:  no bad like she was too lazy to shave her beard but she was in my face
               take my picture take my picture so i did. amazing it turned out ok.
               u shooting pix?
billybatty:    not in the mood.
icdeddpeople:  what mood ru in?
billybatty:    no moods just meds.
icdeddpeople:  hey do u ever miss being crazy?
billybatty:    fuck yeah. not the lows the highs. like when all the trees spoke french.
icdeddpeople:  really??????
billybatty:    no pulled that out of my ass. talk about u. tell me secrets.
icdeddpeople:  um like how much i hate christina agwhatever and her pelvic bones?
billybatty:    lol more more
icdeddpeople:  i wanna go to europe and sit in cafes every day and smoke nonfilters and
               drink stuff that will totally destroy my liver
billybatty:    cool
icdeddpeople:  and pretend I'm not american. is that stupid?
billybatty:    to pretend you're not american? no that's smart
icdeddpeople:  asshole stop laughing at me
billybatty:    no you should go. seriously you've never been?
icdeddpeople:  i've been nowhere no fucking where
billybatty:    your parents never took u?
icdeddpeople:  hello claire fisher dead father space mother middle middle class mortuary girl.
               the only place my dad ever went was vietnam. they took u?
billybatty:    four times
icdeddpeople:  u suck. kidding. well maybe not.
billybatty:    it was hell. except i got to piss in the street. and on some buildings.
icdeddpeople:  hell in EUROPE I don't think so
billybatty:    hello billy chenowith son of margaret and bern hell in any language
icdeddpeople:  at least a different world
billybatty:    different world same shit
icdeddpeople:  wait-mom-
billybatty:    tell ruth I want to sleep in her hair
               lalalalalalalalalalalalalalalalalalalalalalalalalalalalal
icdeddpeople:  k back
billybatty:    go to italy first
icdeddpeople:  why
billybatty:    great design bleeding jesus masterpieces every two feet also torture museums
icdeddpeople:  lol u r torturing me!!!!! gotta go
billybatty:    no don't i'll be good
icdeddpeople:  family dinner ugh ugh ugh
billybatty:    shit this was just getting fun
icdeddpeople:  online later?
billybatty:    probably...look for me and fucking save me from myself...
icdeddpeople:  ciao
billybatty:    xxxbilly
```

```
icdeddpeople:  hey u
icdeddpeople:  hello? r u there?
icdeddpeople:  r u in therapy? in the shower? where r u??????
icdeddpeople:  u might as well IM me back I won't give up
icdeddpeople:  HEEEEEEEEEEEEEEEEEEEEEEEEEEEEEEEEEEEEEEEEY
billybatty:    jesus christ stop screaming
icdeddpeople:  there u r
billybatty:    I can't IM all the time like some fucking teenager
billybatty:    hello?
billybatty:    sorry bad day
billybatty:    claire
billybatty:    HEEEEEEEEEEEEEEEEEEEEEEEEEEEEEEEEEEEEEEEEY
icdeddpeople:  my day sucked too don't take it out on me
billybatty:    oh fuck this
icdeddpeople:  fine bye
billybatty:    i think i saw u today
icdeddpeople:  wait i'm playing hearts with some moron from texas named earl
icdeddpeople:  k back kicked earl's butt
billybatty:    were u here this morning
icdeddpeople:  no way i wish
billybatty:    then she was your  doppelganger
icdeddpeople:  really?? cool i have an evil twin
billybatty:    no you're the evil twin
icdeddpeople:  oh right lol
billybatty:    if u ever meet each other one of u must die
icdeddpeople:  no isn't it like if i meet her the doppelganger explodes
billybatty:    oh yeah, fucked up my doppelganger lore
icdeddpeople:  i wonder what my doppelganger's doing tonight...i hope she's not
               sitting on her ass in front of a computer
billybatty:    every time we say doppelganger i want to wear lederhosen
icdeddpeople:  wait i'll grab my dirndl and a giant cow horn thing
billybatty:    claire claire
icdeddpeople:  billybilly
billybatty:    we're finally in touch with our inner von trapps
icdeddpeople:  lolololololololololololol
billybatty:    see? you yodel
icdeddpeople:  this explains everything
billybatty:    the hills are alive and
icdeddpeople:  we're not fishers or chenowiths we're von trapps
billybatty:    high on a hill lives a lonely goatherd
icdeddpeople:  i wish i was an orphan
billybatty:    me 2 but then there'd be nothing to tell the shrink
icdeddpeople:  they are just all OVER me
billybatty:    who would we blame ourselves on
icdeddpeople:  they are in my face and they don't even know me
billybatty:    do we know them
icdeddpeople:  i don't want to know them...big fucking freaks
billybatty:    pissypissy
icdeddpeople:  well sorry i don't get the mood altering drugs
billybatty:    u can have mine
icdeddpeople:  how can your own family not even have a clue about u
billybatty:    they're just people they're all fucked up
icdeddpeople:  they don't see me they don't hear me i'm a ghost in my own house
               which of course is totally fucking ironic
billybatty:    they love us
icdeddpeople:  no it's only words
billybatty:    we love them
icdeddpeople:  not tonight...grrrrrrrrrrrrrrrrrrr...
billybatty:    if u could be anything what would u be
icdeddpeople:  god lemme think—what would u be?
billybatty:    monk
icdeddpeople:  right
billybatty:    seriously
```

```
icdeddpeople: WHY
billybatty:    leave my family leave the world for god and people would come to me
               for answers and i would have them, i would know what to say
               and i would make the pain go away
icdeddpeople: okaaaay...
billybatty:    u want to be a princess
icdeddpeople: oh gross
billybatty:    with crowns and pretty dresses and princes fighting over u
icdeddpeople: that is so not true quit u r creeping me out
billybatty:    ve haff vays of mekking u tawk...
icdeddpeople: jesus it's hard enough to be myself i can't even think about being somebody else
billybatty:    yeah...just a game...i gotta get outa here i gotta get in the world again
icdeddpeople: believe me u r not missing anything
billybatty:    u don't know...yes i am...i am missing it all
icdeddpeople: u'll be out soon right?
billybatty:    doesn't feel like soon
icdeddpeople: the world isn't going anywhere we are waiting for u to come back and take
               incredible pictures of world weirdness
billybatty:    i don't even fucking care about pictures i just want to be alive
billybatty:    who's the craziest fisher?
icdeddpeople: oh man that is a really hard question the competition is fierce
billybatty:    lol try
icdeddpeople: well i was going to say mom but she's not really crazy she's like loony—
               what about chenowiths?
billybatty:    well i was gonna say me but maybe margaret
icdeddpeople: excuse me but i vote for your sister i mean i like her and she's cool
               but she's crazy and she makes nate totally wacko—well he has his own strange trip
               that's not her fault but sometimes he's talking on the phone with her and
               his eyes go nuts and i think he's gonna foam at the mouth
billybatty:    yeah but brenda can work it, it's like part of her persona thing, sexy u know.
               my mother is just insane and doesn't fucking care
icdeddpeople: david's pretty messed up mostly the gay stuff he was so bitchy today
               it was funny, he doesn't really hurt anybody he's a good guy
billybatty:    bern is just out of it—if he ever came off his cloud and had to deal with his shit—
               well he couldn't he can't
icdeddpeople: we should have been raised by wolves
billybatty:    we kinda were
icdeddpeople: i'm not shy with u here but i'm shy when i see u...not that i ever see u
billybatty:    me 2 kinda but it makes sense
icdeddpeople: no it doesn't it's stupid why does it make sense
billybatty:    here is safe real life is not
icdeddpeople: i wouldn't be safe with u in real life?
billybatty:    I'M not safe with me in real life
icdeddpeople: how can it not be safe? i mean i feel like i really know u
billybatty:    we only ever know parts of people
icdeddpeople: that sucks
billybatty:    don't think so much it fucks things up
icdeddpeople: do u ever lie to me
billybatty:    everybody lies
icdeddpeople: yeah but everybody doesn't lie to everybody
billybatty:    i don't lie to u here
icdeddpeople: once u get out it will never be the same.
billybatty:    maybe it'll be better
icdeddpeople: u know we will never talk in real life the way we do online
billybatty:    at least we talked this way somewhere
icdeddpeople: yeah
billybatty:    that counts
icdeddpeople: yeah but fuck
billybatty:    it counts claire i won't forget
icdeddpeople: maybe...oh well...
billybatty:    xxxbilly
icdeddpeople: xxxclaire
```

It's, uh, it's what Billy does.
He takes pictures of people when they're off guard.
He's got a talent. It's art. ~ BRENDA

No, it's FUCKED! ~ NATE

NATHANIEL
1983

HEAD INJURY / HEAD PAIN / HEADACHE
Hospital General Records and Patient History

DATE: __8/10__   AGE: _____   SEX: M / F

PATIENT'S NAME: __Nathaniel Fisher__

DIFFERENTIAL DIAGNOSIS AND/OR HIGH RISKS:

[]VISUAL DISTURBANCES   []SEIZURE
[]GAIT DISTRUBANCE   []NAUSEA
[]PARESTHESIAS   []PALPITATIONS
[]SHORTNESS OF BREATH   []COUGH
[]FEVER   []SYNCOPE
[]SMOKING   []STRESSS
[]PHOTOPHOBIA   []NECK PAIN

REVISED MRI SCORE

	P/H	A				D/C	
GLASGOW	13-15	4	4	4	4	4	
COMA	9-12	3	3	3	3	3	
SCALE	6-8	2	2	2	2	2	
	4-5	1	1	1	1	1	
	0-3	0	0	0	0	0	
RESPIRATORY	10-29	4	4	4	4	4	
RATE	>29	3	3	3	3	3	
	6-9	2	2	2	2	2	
	1-5	1	1	1	1	1	
	0	0	0	0	0	0	
SYSTOLIC	>89	4	4	4	4	4	
BLOOD	76-89	3	3	3	3	3	
PRESSURE	50-75	2	2	2	2	2	
	1-49	1	1	1	1	1	
	0	0	0	0	0	0	

TOTAL REVISED MRI SCORE

GLASGOW COMA SCALE (Adult / Pediatric)

	P/H	A				D/C
Eye Opening						
Opens spontaneously / Opens spontaneously	4	4	4		4	4
Opens to verbal command / Opens to speech	3	3	3		3	3
Opens to pain / Opens to pain	2	2	2		2	2
No response / No response	1	1	1		1	1
Best Motor Response						
To Verbal Command	6	6	6		6	6
Obeys verbal command / nl. spont. movements						
To Painful Stimuli	5	5	5		5	5
Localizes pain / Withdraws to touch	4	4	4		4	4
Flexion-withdrawal / Withdraws to pain	3	3	3		3	3
Abnormal flexion / Abnormal flexion	2	2	2		2	2
Abnormal Extension /Abnormal extension	1	1	1		1	1
No response / No response						
Best Verbal Response	5	5	5		5	5
Oriented and converses / Coos, babbles	4	4	4		4	4
Disoriented and converses / Irritable crying	3	3	3		3	3
Inappropriate words / Cries to pain	2	2	2		2	2
Incomprehensible sounds / Moans to pain	1	1	1		1	1
No response / No response						

TOTAL GLASGOW COMA SCORE (3-15)

DIFFERENTIAL DIAGNOSIS AND/OR HIGH RISKS:

MRITIC   HEADACHE WITH: (Subdural hematoma, Epidural hematoma, Subarachnoid hemorrhage, PostMRItic headache).
Tension headache, Migraine headache, Cluster headache, Hypertensive headache, Post lumbar puncture headache.
Subarachnoid hemorrhage, Meningitis, CVA, Tumor, Temporal arteritis, Sinusitis, Pseudotumor cerebri, Cerebral aneurysm, Uremia,

                                                        []MENTAL STATUS CHANGES

[]MYALGIA   []ARTHRALGIA

[]SLOW ONSET OF HEADACHE WITH PROGRESSIVE WORSENING.
[]HEADACHE BEGAN WITH EXERTION: []STRAINING []COUGH []SEXUAL ACTIVITY []OTHER _____

_____ READ BY []ED PHYSICIAN []CARDIOLOGIST []OTHER _____
_____ READ BY []ED PHYSICIAN []RADIOLOGIST []OTHER _____
_____ READ BY []ED PHYSICIAN []RADIOLOGIST []OTHER _____

[]EKG: _____
[]SKULL X RAY: _____
[]CT SCAN / MRI HEAD: _____

Encephalitis, Cervical strain, Carbon monoxide poisoning, Eye strain, Glaucoma.

NOTES

PATIENT MRI REVEALS AN (AVM): ARTERIAL VIENOUS MALFORMATION
The definition of the target volume is shown in Fig. 1. The therapist can define the target volume either on the
original (MRI, PC, T1-, or T2-weighted) images (Fig. 1a) or on maximum intensity projection (MIP) images at axial,
sagittal, or frontal projections (Fig. 1b). After target volume definition the dose calculation can be performed
on the basis of AVM MRI data. The 80% isodose lines are indicated as circles in Fig. 1b.

_____   Date _____

_____
Physician's Signature

_____
Print Physician's Name

.49304   .49304
.49304   .49482   .49482

NAME: NATHANIEL SAMUEL FISHER JR.
ADDRESS: 2302 WEST 25TH ST.
LOS ANGELES, CA 90018
PHONE: (213) 555-0012
SEX: MALE
AGE: 35
PATIENT ID: 02-0984
WEIGHT: 163 LBS.
NATIONALITY: CAUCASIAN

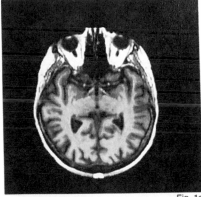

Fig. 1a

MEDICAL HISTORY:	08-38- M CA
AGENT/AGENCY:	CA/PAUL KASA
EXAMINER:	CA/AMERICAN PARA
TICKET NUMBER:	394093990
INS TYPE/AMT:	IND LIFE/$ 150,000
DATE PERFORMED:	10-19-94 XWS 29384
INSURANCE KEY:	3938498902-95
D/T LAST MEAL:	10-29-94 10:30 AM
D/T COLLECTED:	10-29-94 10:30 AM
CERUM APPEAR:	NORMAL
PATIENT ID:	02-0984

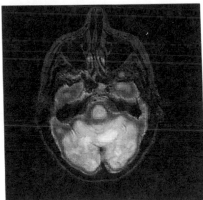

Fig. 1b

MRI TEST RESULTS: MRI REVEALS AN (AVM)
ARTERIAL VIENOUS MALFORMATION

The definition of the target volume is shown in Fig. 1. The therapist can define the target volume either on the original (MRI, PC, T1-, or T2-weighted) images (Fig. 1a) or on maximum intensity projection (MIP) images at axial, sagittal, or frontal projections (Fig. 1b). After target volume definition the dose calculation can be performed on the basis of AVM MRI data. The 80% isodose lines are indicated as circles in Fig. 1b. For each patient MRI was compared with available conventional brain angiograms.

The AVM's were assessed for the size of the nidus, the origin of the feeding arteries and the pattern of venous drainage.

PHYSICIAN'S NAME: B. DiPaolo, M.D.

N. FISHER >>>>>>>>>003858-A7 [288712] PER FILE - REF 201

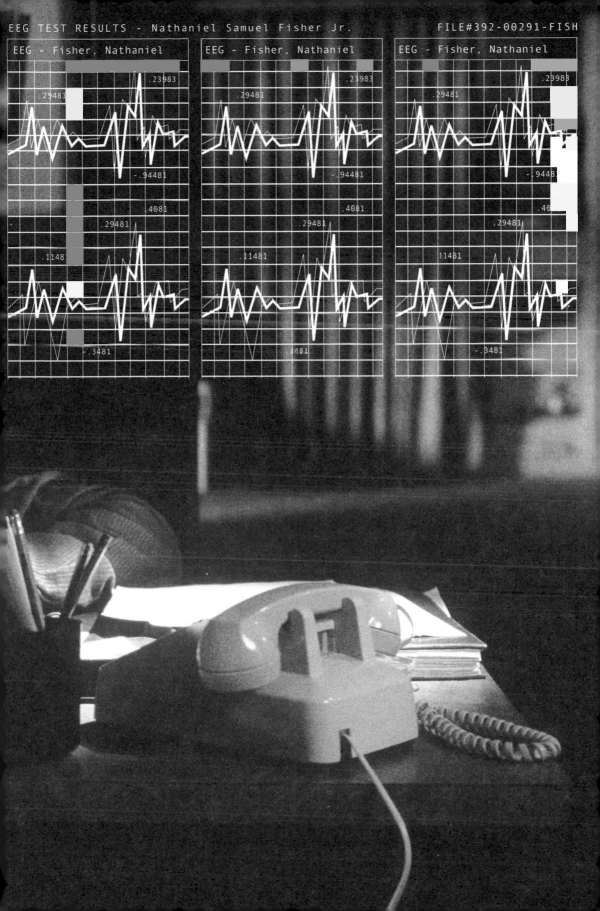

#1 National Bestseller

Your Brother's a Wacko and your Fiancé is going to Die

Dr. Dan Ruderman

2002 | THE STRESS OF BILLY'S MENTAL ILLNESS AND NATE'S DIAGNOSIS TAKES ITS TOLL ON BRENDA'S IMAGINATION.

Maybe it's another Tuesday. Maybe. But this part is undeniably not a maybe: There is nothing to do, nothing. So Christina does what she always does, sits on her porch perch to watch the Venice parade: yoga-bound assholes with fabulous posture, low-slung, hundred-dollar velveteen sweatpants, blonde mom with dog and stroller, two blonde moms, nanny with stroller, homeless guy, homeless guy, surfer boys. . . .

This dude 'n' his buddy. My buddy and I. Why do surfer boys always call each other "buddy"? Muh buddy 'n' I, muhbuddnyI were up at Pismo, muh-buddy-n-I smoked some bowls 'n' surfed some tubes and snowboarded some snow bowls on old-style long boards, goofyfoot. Brainless, long curly hair dancing in their eyes, black lashed, adorable, so moist and juicy they almost reminded her of women.

Her porch perch is her bird's-eye cat seat at a beauty pageant, Mr. Azure and Gold California Beach Boy, Mr. Santa Barbara Redondo Long Beach Huntington Mission Viejo, board shorts hanging down past those lines. What are those lines called? Those inverted L's at the hip bones that frame the cock, upside down, backward L's—pointers on each side of their curved round bellies, tiny baby beer bellies, golden golden boys, blue waves behind them on their movie-screen horizons, Gwen Stefani music heralding their every entrance.

Christina looks up and down and then up again as she pretends to read the weekly political-not rag of the week, restaurant ads, glance up, what's on parade in Venice today? Glance down, bed delivery ads, glance up, sip coffee, we can have your mattress there in less than twenty-four hours, sip coffee, 2-for-1 Tandoori buffet, look up, look down, laser vaginal reconstruction, come in for free consultation, sip coffee, look up, THERE:

On their bikes, these boys, Christina has seen them before, maybe 19 years old, maybe 23 years old. Who cares, they are at least and most long lifetimes younger than her million already lifetimes. They approach her, laser sparkle twinkle eyes, green-blue surf water eyes zooming at her.

As one thing, a pair or pack, together, that's how they see her, Christina thinks, all sunglasses and blown smoke and newspaper. What are they saying as they ride in ever closer circles, circles closing in on her? I'll take her? You can have her? She's mine? She's yours? Let's both? Let's both do her? She's a both? She's old? She's young? She's hot? She's not? She's a slut, she wants it, let's see if we can get some weed off her? I smell pot, is she smoking a joint? That hot cunt, that dumb cunt, that hot bitch, that sexy hot, I smell pussy—

HERE

At her deck. Christina straightens her back. Pulls tank top.

Strap.

"Hey," says one. "Do you have any idea where the Coffee Bean is around here?"

Like they don't know I don't know they don't know I don't know they live around here, Christina thinks. They are always around here, there are a million of them, Troy and Trey and Damon and Dylan, there are forty million of them in California, blonde hair, red hair, blonde-ish reddish, caramel hair, L's pointing, from way down yonder out of the nethers of their board shorts. Turn around, she thinks, turn around so I can see those little half-moons of your ass above your board shorts, Brandon, Brendan, Bryan, Preston, Clayton, Clay, these boys are everywhere here, and they're looking at me, as if they can see me, as if the power of the two of them deciding what I am could even begin.

Begin to name me, it never will, don't even. Just show me that part above your board shorts where the hair on your stomach turns into the hair from your cock, show me your ass, get off of your bikes, as you approach me.

"Christina," she says, reaching out her hand, gently, like a lady.

"Devin and CJ," they say, either being both. Devin and CJ, FUCK, Christina thinks, I thought of every single surfer name in the book, I forgot initials, I forgot PJ and DJ and JP and why do initials always need a J to be cool? I forgot Devin and Kevin and Jace and Burkley and Bo, every last one of them, shirtless, bike, lean it against something, stoned for the past ten years.

Christina points the way to the Coffee Bean, thataway, but they have forgotten that they even asked after it. It is clear now that there are two of them, and they are hot, and there is one of her, and she is hot, and there are three of them, and the three of them know that no one is around, neighbors aren't watching, Christina is

Alone.

No one due, her fiancé, Porter, not due till night. It is day, it is afternoon, and they ask after water, it's all fuzzy now, it's not a request. It's a way into the house, and suddenly Christina is caught up with the idea that they are pulling one over on her, or the idea that that is their belief. They decided in unison they would do her together, that one would start, that they would get stoned, that one would pretend to wait in the other room, and then come in. Whatever, however they could take her, they would do this together, gently, as friends, she wants it, she just doesn't know it yet, they decided.

But Christina knows and knew and knows. So she decides to play it out, play the innocent, the stupid girl, who doesn't know any better, it is her story, she decides, I am the star of this story, I will pretend to be naive and see what they do in my presence.

"Sure, come on in, I have water," and Devin and CJ are behind her, don't bother locking their bikes, barely bothering to look at each other.

Clank.

Clink.

Clonk.

Bikes down on the floor of the deck, dropped faster than buttered bowling balls, their eyes toss secret high-fives to each other. Stupid phrases fall like daisies on the slick wooden hallway, so Christina steps on them, barefoot: "Do people call you Christy/Nice house/Killer fireplace/thanks for the water."

It's all words now, words on the floor, flat flowers, and upside down backward L's around cocks, this enticing perfect place for Christina, on her tiny flying carpet of loin lust where she hovers above normal. This place of waiting, succulent waiting, asking herself, Who will close the door? If I close the door Idiot Surfer Fuck #1 and Dork-Ass Surfer Shithead #2 will know I want them to fuck me together, two against one, two on one, and I can't have them know that, I have to let them think they're taking it from me, pulling one over.

CJ or DJ or whoever-the-fuck J looks at the bong on the table. "Can I take a hit?" And Evan or Devin or whoever the fuck uses this as his moment: "We should close the door, right?" He glances at his buddy (muhbuddynI met this chick who just invited us in and next thing you know we were doin' her) and then at Christina who nods, still playing chaste, you guys are here for a bong hit and nothing else. I am here for the delicious waiting. Christina feels herself getting wet as Asswipe #14 and Big Prick #5 exchange glances, they think

They're pulling one over on me, she thinks.

But this is my afternoon, my hours stretched out ahead of me, where surfer boy and surfer boy will kneel above me and sneak glances at each other's surfer cocks—

And now—

Devin is there, right next to Christina. On. The. Couch. Everything. Slow.

"You've got great legs, do you run er workout er what?" Er what? The words on the walls, on the ceiling now, Devin to CJ now: "Check out her legs—"

This is Christina's favorite part—where she is invisible, where it is a conversation between CJ and Devin and Devin and CJ and Christina is invisible—

HAND on leg.

It is Devin's hand on her leg. He is closer now, "Nice tan," or something. How does it go? CJ comes over to the couch and sits on the other side of her and tries the same tactic—

"Great tits," CJ says, and he touches one. Devin touches the other. This is her moment this is my moment this is Christina's moment to either move and stand up WHATTHEFUCK ARE YOU DOING TOUCHING MY TIT? GET THE FUCK OUT

but

she

doesn't, she is quiet and brings a small smile to her lips, a hidden smile that allows them to continue, and they are up and moving out of the living room, one of them pulling her toward the bed down the hallway, the hallway that takes a million years to walk down until the soft

down soft oblivion of her bed, familiar bedspread, these boys don't know me but my bedspread does, she thinks, my bedspread will be safe, my bedspread will witness this for me.

But first, more weed. No weed is ever enough in times like this, until hours, minutes, seconds, backward seconds backed into this day. How did we get here? Christina has been fucking and fucked for hours. It will never ever be enough. She is nowhere near invisible enough yet.

And then. That horrible moment that Christina hates. Christina hates this moment. Christina hates when she is not invisible anymore. Christina suddenly catches sight of herself across the room, staring back at her, trying to determine exactly what she feels at this moment. Fucking nosy little bitch, she thinks, and shuts her eyes. I'm tired of observing what I feel, tired of analyzing it. I'm sick to death of being my own buzz-kill.

Fuck it, I am actually here, in this room, with these boys, so she speaks.

Finally. For the first time since she nodded about some glasses of water, or bongs, help yourself, four decades ago earlier that day.

    While one cock
    Goes in
    And out
    The words
    She barely recognizes the sound of her own voice: "Fuck me harder, surfer boy." Devin does, he gets into it, he hears her, this is the answer. She *does* want it—he told CJ—she wants it. I told you dude, she wants it.
    "Fuck me. Fuck me harder." The rest, in her head only: Fuck me harder, surfer boy, with your fat little crooked cock and your please-tell-me-you're-not-serious shaved balls.
    And then the internal noise starts again. She leaves the room, her body there, her stupid-smart-too-smart mind off on a tangent again. Why does she have to know so much? And when did straight men start shaving their balls? Does my father shave his balls? Does he like two fingers up his ass like this one does?
    Forget the rest. It went on, the day went on until the sun rose up and fell into the beach waves, crashing, and everyone came, EVERYONE in the entire world came, except, of course, for Christina. She'll come later, after they leave, safe alone with her bedspread, remembering the cock show as a slide show only. For now, she just wants them out.
    One of them. Devin? CJ? Cord? Craig? Sloane? All of them? Did she fuck every surfer in America and Australia and the world that day? He puts on his yin-yang baseball cap and asks for her number as he leaves. "Why?" Christina asks, "So we can date?" His dope-glazed eyes fill with hurt for about half a second, then relief. Men are so fucking consistent.
    And on his way out, he says "Late" in that stupid, surfer way. "Late." Nineteen and already he's a total cliché. Christina feels sad for about half a second, then the familiar relief when she hears the door shut. Why does it always feel so good when they leave?
    Christina is alone, finally. She runs the bath, she needs the bath, she puts the kettle on, she is proud that she did something brave, she never has to tell anyone. This was her afternoon. She was invisible for hours upon hours, and as she gets in the bath, her body will reveal itself to her
    self
    coming up, relief, in the water, her breasts returned as gifts, her pussy, her thighs are hers again. Christina will lie in the water, then lie in the bed, come alone, cum, hand between legs alone, back in the water one more time, to clean and make sure she's really there, and then nap until Porter comes home, and she will make pasta, and they will smile, and he will know nothing of nothing and when he is asleep, ass curved into her stomach for bedtime, she will look at her bedspread.
    She will ball up her bedspread and clutch it, go to sleep.

THE CLARENDON INSTITUTE
RELEASE OF PATIENT AGAINST MEDICAL ADVICE

The release of William Chenowith is effective: December 24, 2001
Authorized by: Dr. Atul Chandrasekar
Dr. Maury Franks

Comments:
At 2 P.M. this afternoon, a woman appeared at the admissions desk wearing a
Santa Claus hat, screaming that she needed to see the doctor in charge. At
first, Debbie R. Joons (nurse on reception duty) thought that she was a potential patient; the individual's behavior was erratic, possibly due to intoxication. The woman looked around the lobby, stating exclamations such as "So this
is the big house." The woman then declared herself to be a psychologist who
could authorize the release of William Chenowith. Nurse Joons verified the iden-
tity of the woman as William Chenowith's mother (Margaret Chenowith), and, as
such, requested authorization to accept and allow her signature for his release.

Originally, I had intended to release William in May 2002. It is my opinion that
he would benefit greatly from six more months of aggressive in-patient therapy
and a closely monitored medication regime. William has, in the past, chosen to
stop medication, which caused a rapid decline into depressive and manic states,
both marked by violent episodes.

Although treatment for William Chenowith has been going marginally well, we need
more time to obtain therapeutic goals. Despite objections of certain staff
members, including Ms. Joons, I believe that the parent demanding release to her
care will be able to perform her duties and that her intoxication is temporary
and only due to pressures of illness of son.

On these three parameters I will allow his release:
1. William returns for 3x per week intensive therapy for 1 month, 2x per week
   thereafter with Dr. Hanover.
2. William agrees to take medication: Lithium 300 mg TID, Risperdal 3mg BID.
3. Family therapy with mother or father 2x month.
4. Cease contact with sister, known to agitate William. It is Dr. Hanover's
   opinion that sister's presence causes in William feelings of helplessness
   and rage.

Accepted by and agreed to: _Atul Chandrasekar_

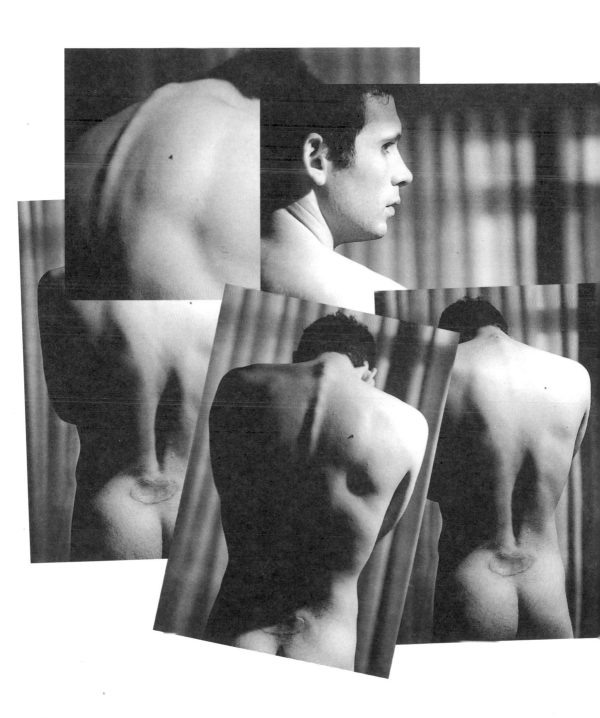

2002 | CLAIRE APPLIES FOR ENTRY TO THE LOS ANGELES COUNTY ARTS COLLEGE.

APPLICATION FOR LAC ARTS

ESSAY 1:

PLEASE ELABORATE ON YOUR REASONS FOR HAVING CHOSEN LOS ANGELES COUNTY ARTS COLLEGE. ILLUMINATE YOUR REASONS FOR BECOMING AN ARTIST, GIVING US AN IDEA OF WHO AND WHAT HAS INFLUENCED YOU SO FAR.

Why do I want to be an artist? In a way, I feel as if that question is absurd, in that, if I could answer it, I wouldn't be an artist. There are no answers, no explanation. There is no figuring it out. There is just the simple truth that I know I am an artist.

I am an artist because I search for beauty in all things, knowing, however, that beauty is not only found in things that are considered, by most people, actually beautiful. It can be found in the dark as well as in the light. Personally, I find myself searching for meaning in all parts of life. While many people experience life from within it, I have at times felt more like a translator from another universe. This is a feeling that, in the past, made me feel so incredibly different from most of my peers, but upon realizing that I was an artist, made me feel completely certain of where this outlook was coming from.

Of course, besides the more pensive ideas about my inner feelings toward art itself, there are the physical realities: the incredibly inspiring Lac Arts campus in and of itself. The moment I saw the campus, with all of the students fully living out their dreams of what art can be, I became entranced with the feeling that it was a place where I could be myself and learn how to make art that means something to me, and hopefully, to other people. I was completely spellbound by all of it.

Regarding my own accomplishments as an artist, the first art project I ever took seriously in my own life were some photographs I took of bodies that were ready for burial. I liked taking pictures of dead people because I felt that even though they're often made up and cleaned up, they are, in effect, the truth. In a way, a dead person cannot lie to you. I felt strongly that the photographs I took said things that words couldn't say. When I realized this, I started to think seriously about being an artist.

My influences include my aunt, Sarah O'Connor, who was one of the first people to encourage me and sense that I had something within me that was worth sharing. She's known as a popular muse of '60s artists, such as Andy Warhol and others in the Factory scene. Through my relationship with her I have made acquaintances with very interesting artists including the renowned ceramicist Fiona Kleinshmidt.

I've also been influenced by Billy Chenowith, a well-known Lac Arts alumnus. He taught me that seeing is not the only way to perceive things. I also love the work of everyone from painters such as Gustav Klimt and Edward Hopper to Modigliani, photographers like Cindy Sherman and Nan Goldin, and even the musician Beck. Although he is almost a sacred symbol of popular music, I find his integrity and true awareness of his own voice an inspiration.

As I stated earlier, as an artist, I look for beauty. It is too easy to see beauty in a perfect pattern, smiles and balloons, the bright colors of life that most consider beautiful. However, I want to find beauty in truth, truth that is sometimes black and white, gray, or something you can feel but not see. This is what I want to explore more than anything else in my life, and this is how I answer that question; there are no real reasons why, there is just this hope of mine, that I really am and always will be an artist.

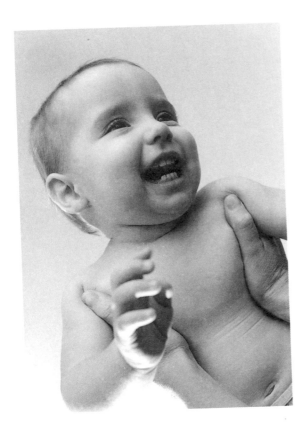

Happy New Year!

Instead of the annual Fisher Christmas letter, I am enclosing this year simply a picture of the most beautiful girl in the world, my new granddaughter, Maya. She is a miracle and a gift (and her Mommy, my daughter-in-law, Lisa, is a good friend to me and a wonderful addition to our family). Please join us in wishing this darling girl joy, dreams, and big opportunities, this year and forever.

Peace,
The Fishers

TAO TE CHING

IF YOU REALIZE THAT ALL THINGS CHANGE,
THERE IS NOTHING YOU WILL TRY TO HOLD ON TO.
IF YOU AREN'T AFRAID OF DYING,
THERE IS NOTHING YOU CAN'T ACHIEVE.

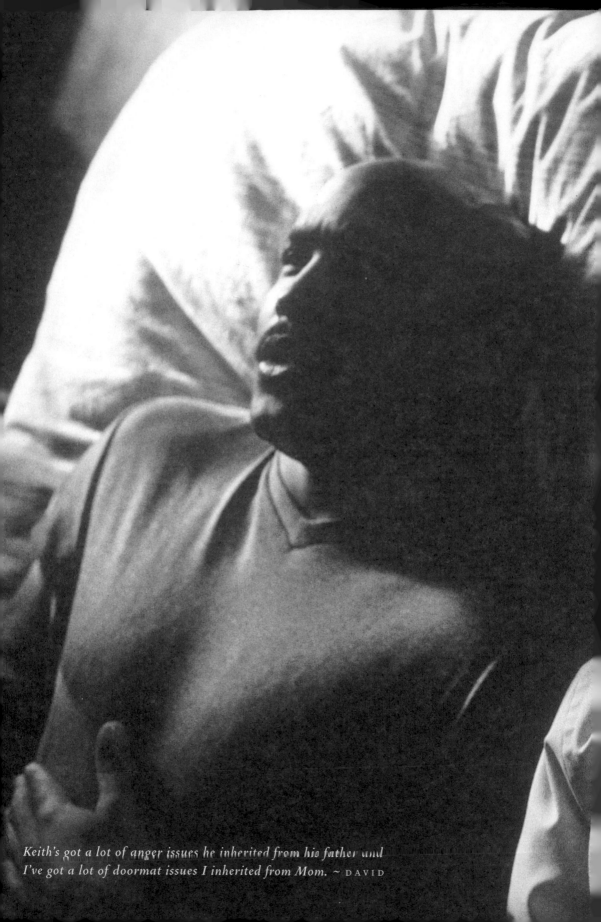

Keith's got a lot of anger issues he inherited from his father and I've got a lot of doormat issues I inherited from Mom. ~ DAVID

GMCLA Newsletter

Only Weekly Publication of the Gay Men's Chorus of Los Angeles

Village at Ed Gould Plaza, 1125 N. McCadden Place, Suite 235 Los Angeles, CA 90038 Phone: **323.467.9741** Fax: **323.46[**

Email: **mailroom@gmcla.org**

Deadline for submissions to the newsletter is 12noon on Monday

dar

arsal @ IPC – 7pm
arsal @ IPC – 7pm
us Retreat @ Camp Hess Kramer

us Retreat @ Camp Hess Kramer
us Retreat @ Camp Hess Kramer
arsal @ IPC – 7pm
arsal @ IPC – 7pm
arsal @ IPC – 7pm
arsal @ IPC – 7pm

Chorus Rehearsal 10am – 1pm
arsal @ IPC – 7pm
ert with South Coast Chorale @ TBA
arsal @ IPC – 7pm
Chorus Rehearsal 2pm – 5pm
arsal @ IPC – 7pm
fit Performance All Saints Pasadena
ired Rehearsal @ IPC – 7pm
s Rehearsal @ Alex – 7pm

White and Blues @ Alex (6:30 call)
White and Blues @ Alex (6:30 call)
White and Blues @ Alex (1:30 call)

rmance in San Diego @ Speckles TBA

= REHEARSALS
REQUIRED REHEARSALS

Good day, good men -

NOTES FROM YOUR ARTISTIC DIRECTOR

Greetings, men!
Welcome back one and all to GMCLA's 25th season. Red White and Blues: An American Music Celebration, which prompted the *L.A. Times* to call us "simply remarkable . . . a cultural treasure," continues to be an unqualified success, with sales of our 10th (and 11th!) compact disc, a 2-CD set of our triumphant concert series, selling on Amazon.com like hotcakes.

We warmly welcome two new members this season, who are filling out the previously thinning ranks in the Tenor section since Bruce Torkington's departure to Tokyo (Bye, Bruce!) and Ken Diamond's move to San Francisco (where he was drafted by SFGMC). David Fisher is a 2nd Tenor and Thommy Hutson is a 1st Tenor. Please introduce yourselves and make them feel like part of the family. Be sure to note the new rehearsal schedule on the back; we continue to meet on Mondays but have also added alternate Thursdays so that we can keep earning those rave reviews! Here's to a glorious Silver Anniversary season,

—Bruce

ANNOUNCEMENTS

George Spain (B1) is looking for a roommate for his 2+2 Craftsman-style bungalow in Silver Lake. Street parking, $800 a month plus utilities. Non-smoker preferred. Must like cats. Please ask George for more info if you're interested or know anyone who might be.

baby doll,
no, i can't fax you the music, you'll have to get it from patrick. trixie
took a dump all over page 2 which fortunately i already memorized.
hey, do these paintball bruises EVER go away? mine (from crawling around
trying to escape your vicious feral husband) are still the size of
detroit and now they're turning green and yellow, colors which are not
in my palette, I'm a winter.
if you don't tell me more about the sarge escapade our friendship is over.

FROM: dfisher4273
TO: songstud71
Have you and Trixie ever thought about couples counseling? I can give you
Frank's number.
I already told you about Sarge, I've almost forgotten about the whole
thing. Gotta go, another viewing. Are we still on for drinks after rehearsal?

FROM: songstud71
TO: dfisher4273
I've almost forgotten about the whole thing.
oh you are such a big fat liar!!! puh-LEEZE. who forgets a three-dick night
except for a porn star which let's face it you are so not. and i mean
that in the nicest way.
what did he say? who did what? was sarge as big, dumb and hot as he looked?
those arms, those shoulders, take me now. what was he like? what did
keith do? has it changed your life forever? did you discover new and exciting
activities you can share with others?
stop making it so difficult for me to live vicariously. do you hate me
because I'm beautiful?
i want details! i want the dvd!

FROM: dfisher4273
TO: songstud71
God, it was a private sexual experience, I am not going to tell you every
little thing. I couldn't even if I wanted to. As I'm sure you well know, when
it's going on, you're in it, you're not watching it so you can report to
your annoying friends.
Yes, Sarge was hot, he was really really hot. He smelled great. I don't think
I could have gone through with it if he didn't smell right. He was like a
very large human dog. Nothing embarrassed him. Nothing. That's so sexy, not
to be self-conscious or watching yourself all the time. I wonder what
it's like.
Of course it was exciting. With three people everything is so much busier.
But also, I don't know, clumsy? We all fell off the bed at least once.
so there were times when we were laughing and then it would get intense and
you'd lose track of who was who and what was whose and who was where—okay
that's enough. That's all you get.

It seems like a dream now anyway. I mean I doubt we'll be driving to La
Habra to do it again. Now LET IT GO.
You still haven't told me if we're going out after rehearsal.

FROM: songstud71
TO: dfisher4273
oh fuck rehearsal. I'm not through being annoying yet.
you know you're really lucky you had your first three-way with a studly
paintball hero. some less fortunate people whose names we will not mention
have woken up in the dawn to discover a troll and a princess tiny meat
drooling on the 300-thread-count pillow shams. now that is painful.
you haven't said a goddamn word about keith and what he thought about it.
this is what fascinates me about three-ways, especially when two are a
couple, the wiggy dynamics. have you even talked about it? what does he say?
i can't believe you don't want more!!! life is so unfair. i can't let
this go. It's all i have to hang onto during this hideously boring day.

FROM: dfisher4273
TO: songstud71
We haven't talked about it. There's nothing to talk about. It was an
experiment.

FROM: songstud71
TO: dfisher4273
oh right. uh-huh. kill me.

FROM: dfisher4273
TO: songstud71
Okay, he definitely liked it. And he was more comfortable with it than I
was. And maybe it was more his idea than mine. So what? We never feel the
same about anything anyway.

FROM: songstud71
TO: dfisher4273
when i was imprisoned in that relationship with Laurence the professor?
we did a trio with a totally shit-for-brains underwear model named Rocco and
the two of them ended up running away to pasadena together. for me, it was
a godsend, but you have to watch your ass with the spices, you know what
i mean?

FROM: dfisher4273
TO: songstud71
WE DID IT IT'S OVER SHUT THE FUCK UP!

FROM: songstud71
TO: dfisher4273
temper temper . . .

CYPRESS COLLEGE

Professional Funeral Service Education Since 1967

ALUMNI PROFILE

Spring 2003

FEDERICO DIAZ: MAKING IT

Federico Diaz proves that you don't have to be what they tell you to be. "Rico" (A.A. '97) grew up in the mid-Wilshire district of Los Angeles, where his father worked in construction. In his parents' minds, he was destined to grow up and join the ranks of the construction industry. "I never really knew what I wanted to do until my dad died. Then when I saw what Mr. Fisher did with my father's body, how he made my father look like a king, that's when I knew," Rico says.

Although his mother was encouraging, his uncle was dead set against his pursuing the career path of a mortician. His uncle told him, "No nephew of mine will spend their days putting makeup on dead people." The cost also made it seem impossible. "We were not wealthy," Rico recalls. Despite these odds, Rico, with the support of Nathaniel Fisher of Fisher & Sons Funeral Home, eventually earned his Associate of Arts degree from Cypress College. "That was one of the proudest days of my life," Rico says, beaming.

Rico has been putting his mortuary science degree to good use for six years now. "A deep appreciation for the beauty of the human body," is what Rico says, when asked what a person must have in order to make it as a mortician. "Plus the dedication to hone your craft. It's not a stretch to say this is a kind of art, what I do."

Today, Rico is living the American dream. He, his wife, Vanessa, and their two sons, Julio and Augusto, reside in L.A., where he is a partner at the Fisher & Diaz Funeral Home.

Fisher & Diaz

Federico Diaz
Funeral Director FDR#B682

2302 W. 25th Street, Los Angeles, CA 90028
Ph 323.555.0164 – Fax 323.555.0168

Fisher & Diaz

David Fisher
Funeral Director FDR#B671

2302 W. 25th Street, Los Angeles, C
Ph 323 555.0164 – Fax 323.555.0168, F

Fisher & Diaz

Nathaniel Fisher Jr
Funeral Director. FDR#B692

2302 W. 25th Street, Los Angeles, CA 9
Ph 323.555.0164 – Fax 323 555 0168, FD#B651

*You can't expect everything to be perfect all the time,
and you can't get shaken when it isn't. If there's a moment
when it feels like you're in prison, you just have to think
of all those other moments when it feels safe. And remind yourself
that those moments outweigh the prison moments.* ~ NATE

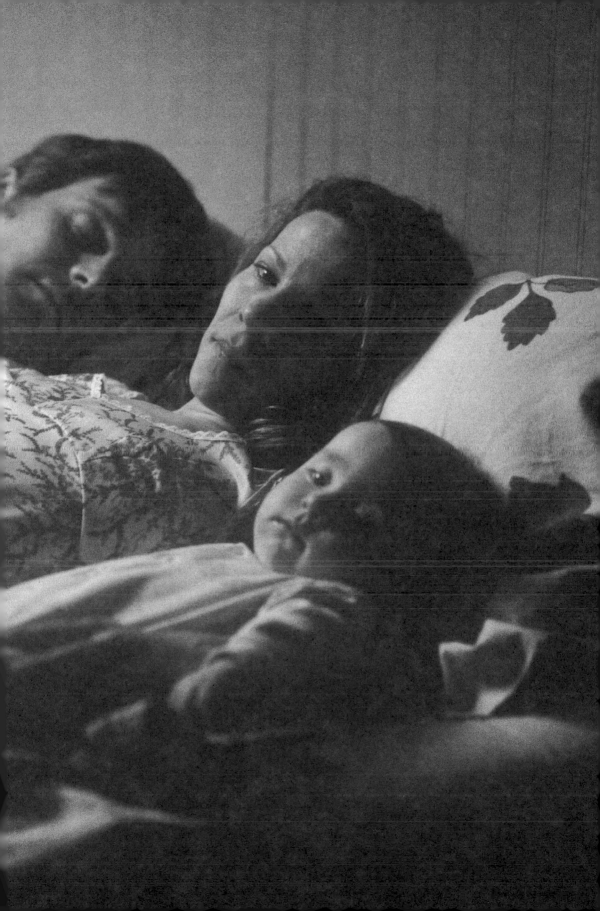

2003 | BRENDA AND BILLY'S PSYCHOLOGIST MOTHER, MARGARET, TAKES NOTES ON HER PATIENTS.

9:00 AM:
Performed Records Review for CA psych association. Boring!!!

10:00 AM:
MK no longer responding well to Paxil—says he misses his "woodies"—requested switching to Celexa—done—but sincerely doubt it will help with "WOODIES." Mentioned suicide twice.

11:00 AM:
CH continues to bring Jungian text to sessions, quoting at length—I advised once more against the counterproductive nonsense but to no avail—asked to borrow the book, but I will not give it back. Must regain control of this one.

12:00 PM:
Lunch with Bern at hospital. Not good. Called Bren and Billy from the room. Bern sobbed, threw up the little jello he'd gotten down. what the fuck is happening to My life...?

2:00 PM:
HJ "cancelled"—then his "wife" showed up instead. claims HJ calls out my name when they have sex—told her i wasn't aware she and HJ had sex—only then did she send the THREE CHILDREN out of the room! Moments later, HJ shows up—they reconcile in front of me and he starts groping her?! Threw them OUT!

3:00 PM:
Interview with prospective patient DG—56 year old male reports feeling "empty"—"aimless"—"like a big nothing"—general abulia—plan for six-week observation and testing with weekly sessions. (Liked his last movie).

4:00 PM:
MS still bereft 1 year after loss of husband—(is this what i have to look forward to? Does Bern mean that much to me? Does anyone?) suspect anorexia-bulimia considering shocking weight loss — referred her to C. De Los Heros for consult. Can't take it.

5:00 PM:
Prepped for critique paper on Rational-Emotive Therapy to be presented at CPA in May: way behind—WAY BEHIND— off to hospital again.

March 7, 2003

Dear Bettina,

It seems like you've been gone forever. How are
you? What is Montana like? I've never seen it. Is
your daughter still in jail? I can't imagine what
your life is like up there. I hope it's not too
awful, dear. Here's a picture from my birthday
party to remind you--look how happy we all were!
    Shall I fill you in on the news around here?
Nate and Lisa are still weathering that first hard
year of marriage. I think they love each other
very much but they don't know it yet. It's a
little sad to stand outside and watch them
struggle with something that should be so simple.
But we all do...you did it three times! Oh, I'm
terrible, aren't I?
    I've given up trying to follow David's moods.
Sometimes he's almost chirpy, but then he and
Keith must have a fight because all of a sudden
you can't get a word out of him. Claire's going
steady, as far as I can tell. He's a very nice boy
named Russell. I wish he would get his hair cut or
at least wash it, but you can't have everything.
And Maya is the sweetest little moonface pumpkin.
    As for me, there have been a few changes. You
remember Arthur, the intern? Well, it's the oddest
thing. It turns out we have an awful lot in
common. You said he wasn't eye candy and he's not,
but he has wonderful qualities and old-fashioned
manners. It's so refreshing. We hang out together,
as Claire would say. I can hear you laughing at me
all the way from Montana. Go ahead, I'm laughing,
too. Life is strange, isn't it?
    Speaking of strange, my sister called. She
sounded happy, so she's either on drugs or not on
drugs.
    I miss you very much, Bettina. Please take
good care of yourself, write when you can and come
back soon.

Your loving friend,

Ruth

Bettina Schm...
204 Wildflower Drive
Pinesdale, MT 59841

March 12, 2003

Dear Ruth,

Do you realize that three quarters of your letter was about other people? And then I got a few measly sentences about you and Arthur. What are you thinking? It's supposed to be the other way around! There'd better be a lot more personal information in your next letter, thank you very much. I need all the laughs I can get.

Just finished my second beer and have to write fast while the kids take a nap, poor mutts. They're kinda fun, actually. They don't deserve their crazy parents. Well, none of us did. I have instructions to pray with them and read the Bible about eight hours a day — I don't think so.

Montana. What can I say about Montana? Here I am in a double-wide trailer in a town of maybe 2000 and 1789 of them are religious fanatics with guns. We also have a lot of dinosaur carcasses up here and it's no secret to me any more ~~while~~ why they died: mass suicide from boredom. The country's beautiful but Jesus Christ, there is nothing to do. Most days the kids and I run around and chase sheep. Once in a while the sheep chase us back and that's our big fun.

My daughter's still in the slammer up the road at a work farm and her husband's locked up the next town over. It oughta break my heart when I see her through a fence or in a smelly visiting room, but to tell you the truth I'm relieved. At least she's healthy and can't hurt anybody. She's not really violent but that cult she's in, they get pretty worked up about Satan and of course everybody's Satanic except them so they shoot up some little Baptist church in the middle of the night and even though nobody gets hurt, you just can't do that.

The people up here who aren't religious fanatics are okay, you'd like them. A few of us play poker and smoke cigars a couple times a week. And there's a good-lookin' old cowboy giving me the eye. Wants to teach me how to ride. Ha! I love it. It's not like L.A., I'm a real hot mama by local standards.

Now Ruth, we have to talk about this Arthur business. The same guy we spied on from the stairs? Another mortician? That is just fucked up. Come on! You need to get out of that house and away from your family, you nut. There's a whole world out there, did you forget that? You can't spend the rest of your life cooking and cleaning with corpses in the cellar. And I have to stay in Montana for a while, so you can't wait for me to come and pull you out of the rut. The one thing you can learn from your sister (the certified maniac, I know) is how to have a good time. So quit acting like the Old Widow Fisher and raise some hell.... Oh the little one is howling, gotta run. Miss you!   Love, Betina

You never smile or laugh anymore.
You don't act like you, you act like—
like one of the Fishers.
~ FEDERICO

*I hate my job. I feel like a
loser. Driving around in a
fucking HomeAlert uniform
answering alarms set off by
poodles, sucking up to rich
assholes who make more in
a day than I do in a year.*
~ KEITH

CLAIRE BEGINS DATING HER CLASSMATE, RUSSELL CORWIN.

```
icdeddpeople:   you there?
Justacreep:     Yeah.
icdeddpeople:   what are you doing?
Justacreep:     Just took a nap.
icdeddpeople:   you don't take naps at midnight, that's called going
                to sleep
Justacreep:     No, it was a nap. I never actually sleep.
icdeddpeople:   you a vampire?
Justacreep:     God, I wish. That would explain so much.
icdeddpeople:   maybe you're an angel
Justacreep:     Got no wings. Or soul, for that matter.
icdeddpeople:   you have the sweetest soul I've ever rubbed my
                hands across
Justacreep:     Can I come over?
icdeddpeople:   hurry
> > > > > > > > > > > > > > > > > > > > > > > > > > > > > > > > > > > > > > > > > > > > > > > > > > > > > > > >
icdeddpeople:   what are you doing?
Justacreep:     Sleeping.
icdeddpeople:   you're always sleeping
Justacreep:     Had the greatest dream about you.
icdeddpeople:   what was it?
Justacreep:     Me just walking, and you were like this presence.
icdeddpeople:   huh?
Justacreep:     You were there, but not really there. You had no body.
icdeddpeople:   you hate my body cause I'm fat.
Justacreep:     You're insane. I love your body.
icdeddpeople:   liar.
Justacreep:     I love your body so much I would like to put you in a
                giant bowl and eat you with a spoon.
icdeddpeople:   okay that's just gross
Justacreep:     I can't do this.
icdeddpeople:   do what?
Justacreep:     These IMs. They're too fucking computery. I hate them.
                I write stupid stuff.
icdeddpeople:   no you don't
Justacreep:     Yes, I do. I just said I wanted to eat you with a spoon.
icdeddpeople:   that made me laugh
Justacreep:     I wasn't trying to make you laugh, I was trying to
                make you feel sexy.
icdeddpeople:   okay maybe you're not so good at it
Justacreep:     See?
icdeddpeople:   hold on. phone
Justacreep:     It's me.
icdeddpeople:   it's you?
Justacreep:     Answer the fucking phone!
icdeddpeople:   hey
Justacreep:     Please, no more.
icdeddpeople:   what?
Justacreep:     Instant messages. I want to hear your voice when I talk
                to you.
icdeddpeople:   i'm sitting  at my computer. phone's way over there
Justacreep:     I'm logging off.
icdeddpeople:   you're mean
Justacreep:     CALL ME!
icdeddpeople:   okay, stop yelling
```

FINAL EVALUATION

CLASS: FORM AND SPACE
TEACHER: OLIVIER CASTRO-STAHL
STUDENT: CLAIRE FISHER

Please evaluate the above-named student in the following categories.

COMPREHENSION OF COURSE MATERIAL

What does Claire Fisher comprehend, that is also what I wonder. She reads the books, she completes assignments on time, she asks questions that make sense. This is good, yes, but a sheep could do the same thing. Does she comprehend that the creation of art will require her body and her soul, her past, present and future? That she can hold nothing back or keep anything for herself? It's possible, she has the intelligence, but I don't know, I hope so. When I'm teaching, she nods yes or shakes her head no or sometimes she just sits there with a blank look on her face like all the other students. Whether she really gets it, whether she can feel the truth of my words in her intestines, this is a mystery to me and remains to be seen.

TECHNICAL SKILL

She has made advances here. She no longer uses the brush like she's hitting canvas with a stick. Her sense of color has improved, but her understanding of mass, volume and light is still primitive. She draws well, is no longer such a clumsy puppy with clay, and her objet trouvé constructions are getting better. Photography is still her strongest medium, and there she shows a growing awareness of design and composition, though she needs more depth and variety in her subject matter.

OBJECTIVE CRITIQUE

This is a ridiculous category. There is no place in art for objectivity. I refuse to write anything in this space.

SUBJECTIVE CRITIQUE

Claire Fisher is a frustrating work in progress. She has the curse of potential. When I look at her, I see here is someone who has everything it takes to become the real thing, a real artist. But over and over through the whole semester I observe how she blocks herself with childish thinking and bourgeois beliefs. If she wants to succeed she will have to overcome this and work with all her passion. It's no accident that her best photography is black and white. This is how she views the world, black/white, good/bad, wrong/right. But that is Claire Fisher's limited perception, it is not life. She has two choices: she can continue as she is and end up taking pictures of cats and flowers for greeting cards. Or she can live in reality and make art.

GRADE
Well, she has learned SOMETHING from me and for this she gets an A.

I'd really like to seriously kick back and unwind and forget about the fact I spend my days surrounded by death. ~ NATE

Dear Mr. Fisher,

You don't know me. My father, Joseph Harkness, had his memorial service and burial handled by you and your company last month, but I was unable to attend because I live here in Taiwan, where I teach English. I would have tried to get back for it, but my sister didn't tell me Dad had died until it was too late to buy a reasonably priced ticket.

Since there is no one in here in Taiwan to talk to who knew my father, and since my relations with my sister are strained (read: nonexistent), I wanted to write to share a memory of Dad with you and thank you for caring for his body.

My dad was a man of great compassion. He worked for a company that made aluminum-plated cookware, but he always behaved as if the real work of his life was caring for others. Whenever he passed a needy person in the street, he always gave them money. He brought my sister and me to volunteer at a homeless shelter every Thanksgiving and Christmas. His idea of a holiday was helping someone else. That's just how he was.

The one day I'll never forget was about ten years ago. I walked home from school and found Dad outside the house talking to a man in his 50s or 60s. He was carrying a large dust-broom and had been going door-to-door offering to sweep sidewalks and porches for money. Dad paid him a few bucks to sweep our porch and walk, but had also taken the time to engage the man in conversation—just like Dad. When I walked up, the man was telling dad how he's just been released from the county hospital. He'd been diagnosed with terminal cancer and they couldn't help him, he didn't have insurance, etc. He was living on the street. Dad offered him our guest room, but the man declined. He was too proud. My dad offered to give him the room in exchange for doing odd jobs around the house. I was only thirteen years old and got kind of freaked out by this; but again, the man declined. Before he finally walked off down the block, my dad gave him all the money in his wallet and a long hug.

I followed my dad inside, expecting him to stop in the living room and ask me about my day. But he walked straight through the house and out into the backyard. He sat down at the picnic table and cried and cried. It scared me, watching him through the window, but eventually I went outside and asked him what was the matter. All he could say was, "It's all so sad. It's all so sad." He cried and cried.

This is not a fun or exciting story, but it is true. And I wanted to tell someone, now that he's gone forever. He was a good person.

Thank you so much. Mr. Fisher, for doing the work you do. I'm sure it isn't easy. And please, if you hear from my sister Denise, don't tell her I wrote to you.

Sincerely,

Suzanne Harkness

Suzanne Harkness

FISHER & DIAZ
FUNERAL HOME

Dear Ms. Harkness,

Thanks for sharing your story about your dad. When we lose someone close to us, telling stories about them is an important part of the grieving process.

Your sister Denise, as you probably know, was our main contact while we handled your father's memorial service and interment. She told my brother David and I a lot of similar stories about your dad. He must have been an amazing person.

You should know, though, that she also talked a lot about you, and she seemed very sad about the fact that you two are so rarely in contact.

I know it's none of my business, but I'm sort of always unable to keep a distance from other people and their feelings. It's something I got from my own dad, who was a decent guy in his own right. We lost him just a few years ago, and my life has been insanely different ever since.

By the way, there is still about $1400 outstanding on your account. I only mention this because I know my brother David has sent some late notices to Denise at her Van Nuys address. Between you and me, there's no rush to pay that off. In fact, calling your sister to let her know that she shouldn't worry about it wouldn't be such a bad reason to re-establish contact.

Not my business, I know.

Have fun in Taiwan. I don't know anything about it. Oh, and the little blue marks at the top of this letter are compliments of Maya, my little baby girl who is with me all day today while my wife is on her way to visit *her* sister. Some coincidence, huh?

Sincerely,

Nate Fisher

Nate Fisher

2302 W. 25th Street, Los Angeles, CA 90018 Phone: 323.555.0164 Fax: 323.555.0168

MISSING

JUNE 9, 2003

LISA KIMMEL FISHER
Please call Santa Barbara County Sheriff

MISSING

JUNE 9, 2003

LISA KIMMEL FISHER
Please call Santa Barbara County Sheriff

MISSING

JUNE 9, 2003

LISA KIMMEL FISHER
Please call Santa Barbara County Sheriff

MISSING

JUNE 9, 2003

LISA KIMMEL FISHER
Please call Santa Barbara County Sheriff

2003 | IN JUNE, LISA DRIVES NORTH TO VISIT HER SISTER, BARBARA, IN SANTA CRUZ. SHE NEVER ARRIVES.

MISSING
JUNE 9, 2003

LISA KIMMEL FISHER
Please call Santa Barbara County Sheriff

MISSING
JUNE 9, 2003

LISA KIMMEL FISHER
Please call Santa Barbara County Sheriff

MISSING
JUNE 9, 2003

LISA KIMMEL FISHER
Please call Santa Barbara County Sheriff

MISSING
JUNE 9, 2003

LISA KIMMEL FISHER
Please call Santa Barbara County Sheriff

When I'm with George I feel like life is full of possibility.
And I haven't felt that way in so long I had forgotten what
it feels like, and I don't ever want to forget that again. ~ RUTH

*You should do whatever brings you deeper
into the reality of your life. . . .
Not the life you think you can have,
but the life you've got.* ~ FATHER JACK

The facts of life and dea
live and die, we love and
disappear. And between
we search for meaning,
a record for those who v

remain the same. We
grieve, we breed and
hese essential gravities,
ve our memories, leave
ll remember us.

This book was produced by Melcher Media, Inc., 124 W. 13th Street, New York, NY 10013.

Publisher: Charles Melcher
Editors: Lia Ronnen and Duncan Bock
Publishing Manager: Bonnie Eldon
Production Director: Andrea Hirsh
Associate Editor: Megan Worman
Photo Researcher: Amy Pastan
Line Editor: David Cashion
Editorial Assistant: Ritsuko Okumura

Designed by Design M/W

Special thanks to: Chris Albrecht, Alexandra Alter, David Brown, Tom Bozzelli, Louise Burke, Rick Cleveland, Bree Conover, Courtney Covington, Adam de Havenon, Robert Del Valle, Max Dickstein, Yael Eisele, Martin Felli, Mike Garcia, GMCLA, Miranda Heller, Suzuki Ingerslev, David Janollari, Christina Jokanovich, Ann Kanter, Bruce Eric Kaplan, Leah King, Laura Kotcharian, Thomas Lynch, John Meils, Pete Megler, Kaitelyn Mercer, Allison Murray, Richard Oren, Jeffrey Peters, Kate Robin, Annie Schaffheitle, Russell Schwartz, Ira Silverberg, Faye Spano, Kara Stanford, Carolyn Strauss, Lorenzo de Stefano, Bobby Thomas, Debra Weintraub, Winston Wesley, Allison Williams, J.P. Williams, and Gordon Wise.

Writing Credits:
The following piece was written by Alan Ball:
Claire's short story, pages 100-103.

The following pieces were written by Scott Buck:
Nathaniel and Ruth's Vietnam correspondence, pages 16–19; Ruth's letter to Sarah and Sarah's response, page 67; Claire and Nathaniel's car contract, page 108; Claire and Russell's IMs, page 189.

The following pieces were written by Cara DiPaolo:
David's fan letter to Matt Dillon, pages 68–69; David's letters to Russian pen pal, pages 70-71, 74–75; Lisa's secret letter to Nate, page 107; Gary's report on Claire, page 144.

The following pieces were written by Gabe Hudson:
"Dear Phyllis" letter, page 22; Article about Chenowith fire, page 84; Letter from Yale to Brenda, page 85; Rebecca's letter to Claire, page 93; Letter from Nora to Nate, page 104–105; Fisher & Sons ad, page 118; Federico's alumni profile, page 176.

The following pieces were written by Joanna Lovinger:
Ruth's note to her babysitter, page 46; David's report card and note from teacher, page 48; Claire's movie report, page 92; Rico's letters to Nathaniel, pages 96–97; Nate's note to Lisa, page 106; Claire's and Gabe's notes, page 145; GMCLA newsletter, page 175.

The following pieces were written by Nancy Oliver:
Letter from guidance counselor about Nate, page 66; Nate for class president interview, page 73; David's article, pages 130–131; Claire and Billy's IMs, pages 146–149; David and Terry's e-mail exchange, page 174–175; Ruth and Bettina's letters, pages 182–185; Olivier's evaluation of Claire, pages 190–191.

The following pieces were written by Jill Soloway:
Lisa's column in Co-op newsletter, page 98; Brenda's novel in progress, pages 158–161; Billy's psychiatric release form, page 162; Claire's college application, page 165.

The following pieces were written by Craig Wright:
"Dear Phyllis" response, page 22; letter from J. Umstead to Nathaniel, page 36; Nathaniel's response to J. Umstead, page 37; Ruth's 1968 Christmas letter, pages 32–33; *Nathaniel and Isabel* story, pages 41–45; Brenda's childhood poetry, pages 56–57; Excerpts from *Charlotte Light and Dark*, pages 60–65; Nate's Life-Skills Inventory questionnaire and letter from teacher expressing concern, pages 72–73; Letter from Keith's mom and Keith's response, pages 90-91; Ruth's Christmas card, page 166; Margaret's psychiatric notes, page 101, letter from Suzanne Harkness to Nate, page 194; Nate's response to Suzanne Harkness, page 195.

Library of Congress Cataloging-in-Publication data is available upon request.

Printed in China

ISBN: 0-7434-8065-1

First Pocket Books hardcover printing November 2003

10 9 8 7 6 5 4 3 2 1

Pocket Books, a division of Simon & Schuster, Inc., 1230 Avenue of the Americas, New York, N.Y. 10020
Pocket and colophon are registered trademarks of Simon & Schuster, Inc. For information regarding special discounts for bulk purchases, please contact Simon & Schuster Special Sales at 1-800-456-6798 or business@simonandschuster.com

Photography credits:
Page 4: Courtesy of Kohle and Credner, AlltheSky.com; Pages 10-11, 40, 59: HBO; Pages 12, 28: Courtesy of Richard Jenkins; Pages 14-15, 30-31, 47, 50-51, 76-77, 89, 94-95, 114-115, 118-119, 122-123, 125, 126-127, 140-141, 164, 177, 198-199: Grant Peterson/HBO; Pages 16-19: Vietnam photos courtesy of AP/Wide World Photos; Page 17: Los Angeles Times masthead copyright © 2003, Los Angeles Times. Reprinted with permission. Pages 20-21, 86-87: Courtesy of The Walter P. McCall Collection; Page 23: Courtesy of Corbis; Pages 26-27: Courtesy of The Dodge Company; Pages 34, 39: Courtesy of Peter Krause; Pages 34, 49: Courtesy of Michael C. Hall; Page 35, 88, 112-113: Tracy Bennett/HBO; Pages 54-55: Magazine ads circa 1970 courtesy of the National Funeral Directors Association; Page 58, 60, 84, 90, 98, 109, 116-117, 120-121, 124, 128-129, 134, 136-137, 142-143, 150-151, 154-155, 156, 157, 163, 170-171, 180 (bottom), 202-203 (photos of Father Jack, Brenda and Nate, Sarah, Claire and Gabe), 208: Larry Watson/HBO; Pages 78-79: Courtesy of Lauren Ambrose; Pages 99, 130, 166, 167, 172, 174-175, 176, 178-179, 180 (top), 182, 186, 187, 188, 190-191, 192-193, 196-197, 202-203 (photos of David and Keith, Rico, Brenda, Nate and client, Ruth and Maya, Lisa): John Johnson/HBO; Page 147: Will Norton/HBO; Pages 200-201, 203 (photos of Nathaniel and Claire and Ruth's wedding): Peter Iovino/HBO.

Text Credits:
Pages 6-7: Reprinted with permission of Pocket Books, an imprint of Simon & Schuster, from TALES OF POWER by Carlos Castaneda. Copyright © 1974 by Carlos Castaneda; Pages 52-53 and 132-133: From THE TIBETAN BOOK OF LIVING AND DYING by Sogyal Rinpoche, Copyright © 1993 by Rigpa Fellowship, reprinted by permission of Harper Collins Publishers, Inc. Pages 110-111 and 204-205: From BODIES IN MOTION AND AT REST by Thomas Lynch. Copyright © 2000 by Thomas Lynch. Used by permission of W. W. Norton & Company, Inc.; Page 138-139: A GRIEF OBSERVED by C.S. Lewis copyright © C.S. Lewis Pte. Ltd. 1961. Extract reprinted by permission.